"And what if I won't?" Martha asked

"Wouldn't it be simpler if I left now, and we forgot the whole incident?" She took a few steps toward the door.

"Oh, I disagree." Quinn Maxwell smiled. "There is something going on, Ms. Clark, something you seem to know about. And I want an explanation."

"You can't keep me here against my will." Anger rippled through her, closely followed by quivers of fear. Would her story hold up?

"Oh, I don't think you'll refuse to wait," he said.

"Why, what makes you so certain?" she demanded sharply.

"Because you obviously came here tonight for something important, something you were prepared to go to almost any length to get. So make yourself comfortable and try to come up with a good story, because believe me, lady, you'll need it."

JENNIFER TAYLOR, Liverpool-born, still lives in Lancashire, though now in beautiful countryside with her husband and young son and daughter. She is a chartered librarian and worked for the Liverpool City Libraries for many years. She has always written and has cupboards full of unfinished manuscripts to prove it. When she decided to try romance writing, Jennifer found it far more challenging and enjoyable than her other efforts. She manages to fit her writing into her busy schedule of working, running the house and caring for the children. Her books contain a strong element of humor, as she feels laughter is important to a loving relationship.

Books by Jennifer Taylor

HARLEQUIN PRESENTS
1326—A MAGICAL TOUCH

JENNIFER TAYLOR

tender pursuit

Harlequin Books

TORONTO • NEW YORK • LONDON
AMSTERDAM • PARIS • SYDNEY • HAMBURG
STOCKHOLM • ATHENS • TOKYO • MILAN

Harlequin Presents first edition March 1991
ISBN 0-373-11349-8

Original hardcover edition published in 1989
by Mills & Boon Limited

TENDER PURSUIT

CHAPTER ONE

'JUST take your time, Mr Johnson, there's absolutely no hurry.'

With a cool smile Martha sat back in her chair, her green eyes studying the middle-aged man seated opposite. He was so nervous, his hands twitching, his feet shuffling, a nervous tic beating in the corner of his cheek. He'd been in her office nearly fifteen minutes now, yet she still had no idea why he'd come. Forcing herself to appear patient, she waited, her eyes moving on from his agitated face to sweep round the room, taking stock of its comfortable yet businesslike appearance: formality with just a hint of the homely. She'd worked hard on this room, determined to get the right atmosphere, and she'd succeeded. Clients who were visibly nervous soon seemed to settle in this soothing room with its pale grey carpet and lavender walls. Mind you, it didn't seem to be having much effect on this one, though it was doubtful if anything apart from a double dose of tranquillisers would help. Still, she was paid to be patient, so she would wait. Some time, sooner or later, he would come out with the reason he was here.

'Ehhmm, well, it's like this Miss . . . Mrs . . . ehhmm.'

'Ms,' she supplied helpfully, 'Ms Clark, if you don't mind, Mr Johnson. I prefer it.'

'Yes, of course, Ms Clark.' His tongue seemed to trip over the unfamiliar title and he hesitated, making Martha almost sorry that she'd corrected him, but long ago she'd found it was the best way to avoid all those awkward questions about her marital status.

'Well, you see, Ms Clark, it's my wife.'

'Yes?' she said encouragingly. Under cover of the smooth teak desk she snatched a glance at her watch, working out just when to expect the next client. She always made it a rule to leave enough time between appointments to avoid having one client run into another, but at the rate things were progressing that mightn't be possible today. She looked up, putting just the right amount of warmth into her clear green eyes and settling her face into a gently understanding expression. It was a trick which she'd learned to cultivate over the past year, and one which usually paid dividends. It paid off this time, too.

The man's agitation lessened visibly and he sat up a touch straighter, running a hand over his thinning hair.

'It's like this, Ms Clark, I think that my wife is having an affair, and I want you to find out who the other man is.'

'I see. And what do you base your assumption on, Mr Johnson? I mean, you do have something other than the fact that she may have changed her daily routine, taken to doing the laundry on a Wednesday rather than a Monday?' Her voice was warm, silky, just a touch amused but not overly so. She'd heard the same tale so often, seen the same look of horror, the same willingness to believe the worst when, frankly, there was nothing worst to believe! It was surprising what sparked off this reaction in one partner to another: a change of hairdo, a new hobby, walking the dog at nine in the evening instead of ten! Yes, it was surprising, and just a trifle alarming, that years of loyalty could so easily be discarded.

'Of course. Margaret and I have been married for over twenty years now, so I think I can safely say that I know her very well indeed, and recently—well, recently, she's been acting quite out of character.'

'In what way?'

'She's been coming up to town regularly, something she's never done before. She's always been more than happy to stay at home. She has her women's meetings, her church flowers and the house, of course—plenty to keep her busy—but take this week, for instance—she's been up twice. Twice! When I asked her where she'd been, she was very evasive and wouldn't give me a straight answer. And then, of course, there've been the phone calls—wrong numbers, she always says, but last time it happened I listened at the door and it was no wrong number,

I can assure you. She knew who was on the other end of that phone. No, she's having an affair, Ms Clark, I'm convinced of it, and I want you to find out all the details. I . . . I've been told that you're very good and very discreet, which is important. I wouldn't want any of this coming out, you understand; at least, not till it has to.'

He was almost panting when he finished, and Martha gave him a few minutes to compose himself while she made a few soothing, gentle noises.

'You can be quite certain that none of it will be made public Mr Johnson. M. C. Investigations is proud of its reputation for discretion, so you can rest assured. Now, if you'll just give me any information you have about your wife's routine, or even if you have any idea, no matter how vague, where she goes on these trips to town, I can set the wheels in motion.'

She drew a gilt-cased pen out of its teak holder and opened a fresh file, heading the first page with the name 'Margaret Johnson' in a clear bold script. She looked up, one slender eyebrow arched in enquiry.

'Well, actually, the last time she came into town, I followed her. She didn't see me, of course, I made certain of that, but I had to find out where she was going.'

'That was very enterprising of you, Mr Johnson. And where did she go? Do you have an address?' Martha hid a smile, wondering at the fact that so many of her clients discovered these abilities for detection at the drop of a hat. The trouble was that many times they did more harm than good, so she always emphasised the point that she didn't expect them to interfere once she had started an investigation. If too many cooks spoiled the broth, then too many detectives just ruined the clues! It was a plain and simple fact.

The man nodded, feeling in his pocket and drawing out a thin little notebook, turning the pages over one by one with an infinite precision which made Martha want to snatch it from him and flick them open. She stifled the urge. From the outer office came the sound of the door opening and the soft, hushed murmur of voices. Obviously her next client had arrived. She only hoped that Jeannie would have the sense to get him settled in the side room with a cup of coffee till she was free to see him. Clients coming to a private detective agency were always nervous, and, if they were given the chance to really think about their decision to come, they would often cut and run. Although M.C. Investigations was doing nicely, there was no way she could afford to let any prospective client escape too easily!

'Ah, here it is!' Mr Johnson had finally found the page he wanted, and Martha hastily brought her mind back to the business at hand, sliding the pen more securely between her fingers.

'Yes, this is definitely it. Six, The Mews Gardens . . .'

The point of the pen skidded, smudging ink across the paper. She looked up, just the merest flicker of surprise on her delicate oval face. 'Pardon, but did you say Six, The Mews Gardens?'

'Why, yes—is there a problem? I'm sure it's right.'

'No, no, of course not. I just wanted to check I'd heard you correctly.'

She busied herself writing the information down while her mind raced. Surely it was the same address as she'd been given earlier by a different client? He too suspected his wife of having an illicit affair, and had found a scrap of paper with the address in her pocket. What on earth was going on?

Five minutes later she ushered Mr Johnson from her office, then hurried back to her desk and leafed through the small stack of manila folders in her tray to find the one she wanted. She flicked it open, skimming through the details, then paused as she spotted the address. The words seemed to leap from the page at her and she nodded, her brow creased into a tiny puzzled frown. She'd been quite right, it was the same address as she'd been given once before.

She sat down slowly, spreading both files open before her on the desk. Her first client, a Mr Morris, had been thoughtful enough to provide a photograph of his wife, and for several minutes Martha studied the picture of the pleasant-faced, middle-aged woman, her hair neatly permed, her clothes sedately conservative, then compared it with the written description given by Mr

Johnson of his wife. They could have been two peas from the very same pod! She sat back, tapping the end of the pen against her small, even white teeth, more perplexed than ever.

Two women, two middle-aged, respectable ladies, mainstays of their communities . . . so what on earth were they doing sneaking up to town, and to the very same address? Were they really, as their husbands suspected, indulging in illicit affairs? But with the very same man! The idea was intriguing, absorbing enough to demand the personal attention of Martha Clark: Private Investigator. She would deal with both cases . . . herself!

It was so cold. Teeth chattering, Martha started the car, gently revving the engine till it settled into a steady rhythm. She sat back, rubbing her hands briskly together to ease the chilling cramp from her fingers, then picked up the giant-sized thermos flask to pour herself another cup of coffee. A thin trickle of tepid liquid ran out, quarter-filling the small plastic cup, and she bit back a sigh. She was cold, she was hungry, she was tired and she wanted to go home, but she couldn't. This was her third day parked in the road opposite Six, The Mews Gardens, and so far she'd seen absolutely nothing to justify her presence. There had been no sign of life from within the small, smartly painted house, and no sign of anyone coming to visit either. Whoever lived there kept a very low profile, so low that she was beginning to wonder if they existed. Maybe number six was the Mary Celeste of houses, the ghost house where all the occupants mysteriously disappeared, because surely at some point during these three long and infinitely boring days someone should have come in or out!

Disgruntled, she swallowed the lukewarm drink, grimacing at the powdery aftertaste it left in her mouth, then screwed the top firmly back into place. She revved up the engine, turning the heater up to full blast for a few minutes while she stretched her booted feet towards the soothing flow of warm air. A heavy grey dusk was already falling, shrouding the quiet street and cutting down her vision. It wouldn't be worth staying much longer, as soon there would be nothing she could see. This was the part of the job she hated—the long, tedious hours spent just sitting and waiting for something to happen—but it had to be done. In fiction, detectives led glamorous lives, filled with excitement and action but, in reality, it was vastly different. A real detective's greatest asset was patience, but frankly Martha had the feeling hers was being eroded by the minute. If only something would happen, and soon!

She picked up a wad of tissues and wiped the smears of steam from the windscreen before reluctantly aiming the flow of warm air upwards again. She glanced at her watch, easing the cuff of her thick wool jacket and the sleeves of several sweaters away from her waist, and groaned in dismay. Only four o'clock! She'd thought it was much later than that. There was no way she could leave just yet; she would have to stay another hour at least. Still, tomorrow she could get one of the men to come out and take a turn. After all, what did she employ them for if she was the one sitting here, getting bored out of her skull? No, it was just a wicked waste of her talents when there was still that insurance claim which needed winding up and billing. Now, that had been worth taking on, not only for the satisfaction of discovering exactly what had happened to the huge horde of diamonds and pearls which had 'disappeared' when the owner was away, but also for the fee, which promised to be enormous. By her reckonings it should cover the day-to-day expenses of M.C. Investigations for several months to come, and leave a tidy bonus over for her own pocket!

Musing over what to do with the little windfall, Martha settled back in her seat, trying to assess the varying merits of buying a new car or taking a holiday. It was difficult to decide when she could do with both so badly, but it passed the time pleasantly. So lost in thought was she that for a few minutes she failed to register the fact that someone had just walked down the street and stopped outside the door to number six. For a brief moment she stared idly at the woman, then shot bolt upright, as though jolted by a sudden electric current, and peered out through the grey dusk, trying to recognise her.

She was facing the door, her back towards Martha, so that Martha couldn't see her face, just a few stray curls of pale, possibly grey hair, escaping from the bottom of a sensible, knitted hat. Who was she? Margaret Johnson, Elizabeth Morris . . . or someone else?

With a cautious stealth, Martha wound the window down, steeling herself against the sudden blast of freezing air which brought the full joy of a cold December into the car, making her eyes water. She wiped the trickle of moisture from her cheeks and peered out.

The woman knocked at the door, waiting patiently for a few minutes before knocking a second time. She'll be lucky, Martha thought wryly, there's no one there, then nearly bit her tongue as the door was opened just a fraction. So there was someone there, someone who'd not been through that door for three days now. If only she could see who it was . . . but the gap was just too narrow to see who stood in the doorway.

Fired with fresh enthusiasm, she huddled against the car door, straining to hear what was being said, but it was quite impossible at this distance. The best she could manage was a low murmur, a buzz of muted sound which wouldn't shape into words, no matter how hard she tried.

Suddenly a small, feminine laugh assailed her ears, and as Martha watched the woman reached forwards, her hand raised as though touching the other person in a gentle caress before she turned away and the door was swiftly closed. Marthá had just a second to snatch a glance at her face as she hurried past, but it was all she needed to identify the caller as Elizabeth Morris, her first client's wife. She sat back in her seat, her mind racing, suddenly forgetting the cold and discomfort.

So there was something going on, and, if that tender little gesture she'd just witnessed was anything to go by, something Mr Morris wouldn't approve of at all! She smiled, a light of enthusiasm in her green eyes which had been missing for the past few hours. It looked as if she finally had a case, something to get to work on—so now to set the wheels in motion and solve it!

For a few minutes she sat quietly, working out what to do next. Her main task, of course, was to find out the name of the person who lived in the house, and, though she knew she could do that fairly easily by checking the Electoral Register, it would be yet another delay. By the time she got across town, the council offices would be closed, which would mean leaving it until tomorrow. There was no point in doing that, in wasting still more valuable hours when she could—well, she could employ a few sneakier tactics to secure the information she needed. After all, she'd done it before, and successfully, so she might as well do it again.

She ran a hand through her short, tousled, dark curls, fluffing them away from her face, then got out of the car and walked briskly down the street.

She stopped outside number six and lifted the brass lion-head knocker high before thumping it down hard against the plate with a half-dozen or so satisfying thuds which reverberated up and down the quiet street. There was no way the occupant couldn't have heard that. It was enough to waken the dead!

The door swung open and Martha looked up, pinning a nice, firm smile to her lips, ready to begin her little speech . . . only she never got a chance to begin.

'You're late. Come in.'

The voice was low, deep, and filled with so much irritation that she was momentarily struck dumb.

'Oh, for heaven's sake, come in before I catch pneumonia!'

A large, tanned hand shot out, grasping her arm, then she was quickly and ruthlessly hauled inside!

For several seconds Martha stood in the dark hallway, staring down at the fingers locked round her arm. Under other circumstances she might have appreciated the sculpted beauty of that hand with its long, lean fingers and well-shaped nails, but not right now. She was shaking, quivers of fear racing icily up and down her spine, and she drew in a swift, deep breath to steady the tremors before slowly following the hand up to the wrist and beyond.

The wrist was attached to a long, equally tanned, muscular arm, and that in turn was attached to one wide, well-developed and totally bare shoulder. Green eyes widening by the second, Martha swept her gaze up, a long way up, to study the owner of all this bare and powerful flesh, and stifled an unwilling gasp of appreciation!

In the dim light the man's face looked as though it had been carved from golden stone, the cheekbones high, the jaw square, sensuous power in every angular line. Dark gold hair fell over his wide, tanned brow, brushing the curve of thick golden eyebrows, arched over silvery-grey eyes; eyes which were studying her with a less than mutually appreciative expression. In fact, they were studying her with such obvious irritation that Martha hastily took a step backwards, breaking free from his grasp.

'If you're quite ready,' he said with a biting sarcasm which set twin flags of colour into her pale cheeks, 'then we'll begin.'

He walked away down the dimly lit hallway, and Martha stared after him, her eyes huge in her startled face. Apart from a pair of silky dark boxer shorts slung low on his lean hips, he was totally naked, from the tips of his large well-shaped feet to the top of his elegant golden head! She closed her eyes, leaning weakly against the cream-painted wall. What in the name of heaven was going on here? What was she expected to begin?

For several minutes she stayed where she was, legs too weak to support her body, then with a mighty effort she pushed herself away from the solid comfort of the wall. Nothing was going the way she'd anticipated, not that there had been the slightest chance she could ever have anticipated all this in her wildest imaginings! Still, she couldn't afford to let it throw her completely off balance. She had to remember why she had come, and carry through her plan . . . if he would let her.

With stiff, jerky steps she followed the route he'd taken and peered into the room. It was a bedroom, a big one, exquisitely decorated in a purely masculine blend of black and silver, with touches of deep red, and it was empty. She stepped inside, her eyes sliding over the furnishings, taking rapid stock of each item, before halting on the huge, circular bed. Covered in a black silk spread, richly patterned with red and silver embroidery, it was like nothing she'd ever seen outside of a movie, and for several minutes she could only stand and stare at it, till a movement in her side vision brought her abruptly back to her senses.

She glanced round, and felt every drop of blood rush to her head. The man was standing in the part-opened doorway to what was evidently a bathroom, staring down at a small bottle of colourless liquid in his hand. Gone were the shorts now, replaced by a narrow strip of blue towelling which left even less of his powerful golden body to the imagination. He looked up, his eyes still faintly hostile as they noted her rigid stance, then tossed the bottle to her. Martha caught it, her actions purely reflex. She clung to it for a second, like a drowning man to a tiny raft, desperate to put some reality into the whole fantastic situation.

'Right, then. Just let me get comfortable, then we can get started.'

He strode over to the bed, stripping off the silky cover before lying face down, his arms raised above his head, and Martha could only stand and stare at him, transfixed with a dawning horror. Get started! Get started on what? was the question, but she had the strangest feeling that she knew the answer. In stunned silence she stared at his naked back, the powerful curve of his flanks, the muscular line of his strong thighs—and gulped. Case or no case, this was getting way out of hand, above and beyond the call of duty!

With a jerky little movement she tossed the bottle aside and swept from the room, striding quickly along the hall towards the front door and freedom. The sooner she got out of this . . . this den of iniquity, the better!

'Where the hell do you think you're going?'

A large hand caught her once more by the arm, the same hand that had caught her earlier, and she stopped dead, swinging round to face its owner. In the half-light his face was stern, a stiff, uncompromising mask of golden planes and darker shadows, his eyes like twin silvery flames as they burned angrily down at her. She hesitated, fear and some other emotion fighting for precedence inside her.

'Well, I asked you a question, didn't I? So answer me, woman!'

The fear and the other emotion were swept aside by something stronger. Just who did he think he was, manhandling her this way, talking to her like a lackey? Fury ripped through her, and with a swift twist she broke free of his hold, her own eyes sparking with evil green temper. Usually Martha was the most even-tempered of people, able to see every side of a question, to ignore the most irritating traits in friends and acquaintances. She could usually find justification for any and every action, but not this one, definitely not this one! She stood up straighter, her back ramrod stiff as she faced the man across the narrow width of the hallway.

'I, for your information, am going home.'

'What the hell for? You've only just got here.'

'Because there's no way I'm going to stand here and have you or anyone else talk to me like that,' she said coldly.

For a second they glared at each other, not exactly eye to eye when he topped her by a good six inches even in bare feet, but still as equal as she could make it. Then slowly the look of anger faded from his face, to be replaced by just the faintest hint of apology. He hitched the small towel a bit more securely around his hips, and Martha studiously ignored the action, keeping her eyes locked on to the comparative safety of his face and away from his disturbing body.

When he spoke, his voice was low, gruff, as though the words cost him a vast amount of effort by being unfamiliar to him.

'Look, I'm sorry, Miss . . .'

He paused, one thick brow rakishly curved in an enquiry, and Martha unbent just enough to supply the missing information.

'Clark . . . Ms Clark.'

'Ms Clark.' There was no inflection in his voice, no nuance to his deep tones, yet she had the sudden, unshakeable feeling that the title had filled him with amusement. She glanced up, stormy green eyes locking briefly with silver, and saw the fleeting glimpse of it in their depths. Colour flared in her cheeks and she opened her mouth to resume her tirade, but he stepped in quickly.

'Ms Clark, I'm very sorry if my behaviour has upset you in any way, but you have to understand that I'm desperate! I really need your services today . . . so, please, won't you stay and put me out of my misery?'

That was it! He'd gone too far, overstepped the limit by yards, not inches. How dared he? How dared he proposition her that way? The sheer effrontery of the man was so great that for a moment Martha stood transfixed with rage—but only for a moment. Stepping back, she raised her hand and hit him hard across his lean cheek, feeling the force of the blow sting into her palm in a totally satisfying way.

'Why, you little . . .'

Fury shone in his eyes, showed in the sudden coiled tension of his big body, and the satisfaction waned a fraction. Maybe she had been a little bit hasty, a trifle careless in doing that. After all, here she was, alone in the house with him in that state of undress, so maybe it hadn't been the most sensible thing to do in the circumstances. Filled with alarm, Martha tried to push past him, her hands sliding over the warm, hard muscles of his chest, feeling the skin-to-skin contact in every cell of her body.

'Oh, no, you don't! You don't get away that easily!'

He caught her hands, twisting her arms sharply behind her back so that she was forced against his body with a jolt which whooshed the air from her lungs. For a moment he stared down into her startled face, and Martha caught her breath at the expression in his eyes. Time seemed to shudder to a halt as a strange tension gripped them both. Then slowly he dipped his head, his eyes locked to her parted lips, and Martha knew that he was going to kiss her. The strange thing was, there was no thought of resisting in her head. She closed her eyes, feeling the warmth of his breath drift over her skin, waiting for the touch of his lips on hers.

The sound of the knocker beating a rapid tattoo on the door jerked her back to reality with a flourish. She opened her eyes and stared with horror into the face of the tall, golden stranger; a stranger whom she'd been about to kiss with every scrap of feeling in her slender body! Embarrassment flooded through her and she pulled quickly away, turning her face away from his silvery gaze. What on earth had come over her, making her act like that? She lifted her hands, easing the tangle of dark curls away from her hot, flushed cheeks, unable to meet his eyes.

He hesitated, as though wanting to say something, but a second pounding on the front door broke the moment. With a muttered oath he turned away to wrench the door open, but not before Martha had seen the betraying rise and fall of his deep chest. He had been just as affected by what had so nearly happened as she had, and she was glad. Somehow it made her feel just a tiny bit better to know he'd been as shaken by it as she had.

'Yes?' Stiff-legged, he stood in the open doorway, seemingly oblivious to the scantiness of his clothing and the icy wind blowing in from the street. Martha craned her neck to peer past him, her eyes studying the heavy-set woman who stood out on the step.

'Mr Maxwell?' she said, 'I'm Mrs Jones, the masseuse from the Fitness Parlour. I believe you are expecting me.'

She stepped past him into the hall, nodding briefly to Martha, who was still standing exactly where he'd left her, too weak and shaken by all that had happened to move a single inch.

'Shall I go through?' Without waiting for an answer, the woman walked briskly down the hall, her sensible laced shoes clumping heavily against the rich Turkish carpet, peering into each room in turn till she located the bedroom.

They watched her go in silence, then slowly Martha looked up into his face, wondering what was going to happen next. For a second he held her gaze, then slowly, very slowly, closed the door, his hand resting against the lock for several seconds before he turned back to face her.

'If that is the masseuse . . . then just who the hell are you?'

It was the sixty-four-thousand-dollar question, and Martha prayed desperately that she had the answer equal to its value!

CHAPTER TWO

'I . . . I . . .' MARTHA licked her dry lips and tried again, finding it strangely difficult to slip into the role she'd rehearsed such a short time ago in the car. So much had happened in these past few minutes that it felt as though it had been in another lifetime. 'I . . .'

'Mr Maxwell! I'm sorry to interrupt, but I would be grateful if you could come through right away. I'm already running late, and I still have another client to visit tonight.'

The masseuse stood in the bedroom doorway, arms folded across her ample white-overalled bosom, and Martha saw her chance and grabbed it. The stalwart Mrs Jones mightn't be everyone's idea of a good fairy, but she certainly was hers at that moment!

'Look, I can see that you're busy right now,' she said quickly, edging towards the front door, 'so perhaps it would be better if I left.' She smiled at him, a nice, cool little smile, which cost a vast amount of effort, and wavered and flickered like a spent candle when he stepped forwards, pinning her with a steely glance.

'Oh, no, you don't! There's no way you're just walking out of here without some sort of explanation, lady, so you can just hold it right there. You come into my house, pretending to be someone you're not, then calmly think you can just walk on out again. Well, you can think again!'

'I came in?' Suddenly furious at the blatant untruth, Martha rounded on him, her eyes sparking. 'I came in? You mean, you dragged me in, and don't you forget it. The only reason I'm in here is because you made me!'

They squared up to each other like prize fighters, the air between them crackling with tension, then a small, discreet cough broke the silence.

'If you want me to come back another day, maybe tomorrow, if it's not convenient right now——' Mrs Jones was hastily pulling on her coat, an embarrassed flush staining her heavy cheeks.

'No. Tomorrow is no good,' the man said sharply, his eyes flicking briefly in her direction before returning to Martha, as though frightened she would disappear if he didn't watch her. 'I've already had three near sleepless nights because of this pain, and there's no way I want another. I'll be in directly, Mrs Jones, so please wait.'

He waited till the woman had gone reluctantly back into the room before he turned his attention back to Martha, and instinctively she stepped back a pace, feeling suddenly far less brave. In the dim light he looked both angry and tough, and she had a feeling that she would be no match for him in this mood. She had to do something to ease the situation, and get her out of here.

'I really am sorry if I've upset you, but you must agree that it seems to have been just one huge mistake, from start to finish. So, please, won't you just accept my apologies and let us call it a day?'

She forced a conciliatory smile to her lips, holding it rigidly in place as he continued to stare coldly at her. There was silence in the small hallway, then he raised his hands, running his fingers through his hair and down the back of his neck to knead the muscles.

'You're quite right,' he said quietly. 'I'm afraid things just got out of hand. I apologise for my behaviour. I'm not usually so unreasonable, but as I said, I've been in a lot of pain these past few days and it has left me feeling very tense. Allied to that, I've had the strangest feeling that there's been something going on; you know, that funny prickly feeling you get when someone's watching you.'

He smiled at Martha, a wry, self-mocking little smile at his own foolishness—but she didn't feel able to share the joke! She looked away, desperate to hide the alarm which tingled through her at his words, but she was just a shade too slow.

'Why do I get the feeling that rings a bell?' he asked softly, a thread of menace in his deep voice. 'Just what is going on? Why did you come here today?'

He moved closer, and Martha hastily backed

up until her shoulder-blades brushed against the wall. She looked round, her eyes frantic as she searched for some way out, but there was none. He was standing between her and the door; there was no way she could get past him.

'I'm waiting,' he ground out.

'Mr Maxwell, please! I really must ask you to come now or I shall have to leave!'

Mrs Jones stood once more in the doorway, her face set.

'I'll come now,' he answered, his eyes never leaving Martha's pale, strained face. He waited till the masseuse had moved out of sight again before he spoke. 'Right, then, Ms Clark, if Clark really is your name, I think you had better wait in the sitting-room until I'm free.'

He leant over to open the door just to one side of her, his bare arm brushing lightly against her shoulder, and she jerked away from the unwelcome contact. He flicked a switch, bathing the room in a soft golden light, then stood aside with a mocking courtesy for her to enter.

'Make yourself at home. There are drinks on the side table, so help yourself. I won't be long.'

He turned to go, and Martha hastily tried to grab hold of her reeling senses. She couldn't just sit here, waiting meekly till he came back, ready to answer his every question. It was far too dangerous. She had to leave.

'Mr Maxwell,' she said firmly, 'this is just ridiculous. There is no point in me waiting. I have a lot to do and I'm sure you must have too.

Wouldn't it be simpler if I left now, and we forgot the whole incident?'

She took a couple of steps towards the door, halting slowly when he made no move to get out of her way. He just stood there and smiled, if one could call the rather nasty curl of his lips a smile, which was doubtful.

'Oh, I disagree. I think there's every point in your waiting. There is something going on, Ms Clark, something you seem to know about, and I want an explanation. So, please, just for me, won't you wait and make my day?'

'And what if I won't? You can't keep me here against my will!' Anger rippled through her, closely followed by a few cold quivers of fear. Would her story hold up under examination? Suddenly she was less than certain that it would be showerproof, let alone water-tight!

'Refuse to wait. No, I don't think you will do that.'

'Why? What makes you so certain?' she demanded sharply.

'Because you obviously came here tonight for something important, something you were prepared to go to almost any lengths to get. I think you'll wait, but just to be certain, I think I should point out that there's a deadlock on the front door, and that I've taken the precaution of removing the key.' He held his hand out, palm upwards, and Martha just had chance to snatch a glance at the small brass key before he closed his fingers over it with a low, deep laugh.

'Believe me, there's no way you're going to get out of here tonight unless I let you. So make yourself comfortable and try to come up with a good story, because believe me, lady, you need it!'

He closed the door quietly behind him and Martha stared after him, her eyes wide with shock and anger, both at him and at herself. What a mess she'd got herself into; what a terrible, awful mess!

On leaden legs she crossed the room and sat down on the hide-covered sofa, closing her eyes, but that was a mistake. As soon as her lids blotted out her surroundings, the memories returned with a vengeance: memories of those strange tense moments when he had held her in his arms! She groaned, her eyes shooting open to sweep round the room. She just had to find a way out of here, and fast.

The room ran from front to back of the house, with windows at either end, and for a second Martha studied them, her mind racing. Was there just a chance she could climb out of one of those windows and escape? She hurried to check them, but one glance was all she needed to knock that little idea on the head. The windows were quaintly cottage styled and completely charming, but there was no way even a cat could have squeezed through their narrow openings, let alone a person. She would have to think again.

She stared round the room, desperate to find something to help her out of this predicament, but at first glance it wasn't encouraging. It was just a comfortable sitting-room, expensively furnished in an attractive combination of rich brown and palest cream, with the same predominantly masculine air she'd noticed in the bedroom. About half-way down the room, a narrow spiral staircase wound upwards, and for a second Martha's eyes lingered on it, following the twisting curl of cream-painted metal and oaken treads. What was up there? Could there be a way out?

Heart hammering with a renewed surge of hope, she ran across the room and up the stairs, clutching hold of the banister rail as her booted feet slid on the polished treads. At the top there was no landing, the stairs led directly into a room, and she gasped in amazement as she looked round.

The room was huge, encompassing the whole of the upper level of the house, as though several smaller rooms had been knocked together to form it. One side was entirely devoted to a full range of exercise equipment, while the other side was equipped as an office.

Rather stunned by this unexpected discovery, Martha walked slowly across the bare, polished-plank floor and stared at the expensive computer system, the bank of telephones and teleprinters, her green eyes filled with confusion. What on earth did that man need all this highly sophisticated equipment for?

It was a puzzle, all right, but one she knew she

didn't have time to solve at this moment, so she stored it away for later. What she had to concentrate on now was getting out. She glanced round the room and then she saw it—a door, right at the very back; a door which, from its position, could lead nowhere except outside. Could it be some sort of fire escape?

She ran down the room and turned the handle with urgent, shaking fingers, stepping back in amazement when the door opened and a blast of cold air flooded into the room. For a second Martha stood rooted to the spot, so surprised to find it wasn't locked that her brain seized up. Then common sense returned with a flourish. How long had it been since he'd left her? She didn't really know, but instinct warned her that it must nearly be time for the massage to finish. She had to get out of the house!

She stepped out, feeling her spirits sink as she realised that she wasn't on a fire escape as she'd hoped, but on a small stone balcony which overlooked the back garden. How was she ever going to get down from here?

She inched forwards, gripping the cold metal guard rail as she leant over and peered through the misty gloom, trying to assess just how far it was to the ground. It was hard to tell with any degree of accuracy, but it seemed a long way . . . an awful long way, in fact!

Her stomach lurched and she drew back, drinking in breath after breath of air as she tried to stem the waves of panic. If there was one thing which Martha hated above anything, it was heights just like this one: a small square of space suspended above nothing.

Senses reeling, she leant back against the rough brickwork as she tried to find something comfortingly solid to hang on to. Cold, dank night air swirled round, chilling her body, yet she could feel the perspiration trickling between her shoulderblades. She closed her eyes, willing the attack to pass, and in that instant heard the unmistakable sounds of movement from within the house. They had finished!

Her eyes shot open and she swallowed hard to ease the choking knot of tension from her dry throat. It was now or never. She must either pluck up enough courage to make the climb down from this balcony, or she must stay and face that man, Maxwell. It was a hard choice, but something told her the climb could be the lesser of two very nasty evils.

She crept forwards once again and leant over the rail, fighting down the nausea with a grim determination. She would get out of here even if it kill—— Her mind snapped shut on the rest of that little idea!

A heavy wooden trellis was fixed to the wall just below the balcony, its diamond pattern supporting the winter-dead remains of an old climbing rose tree, and for a second Martha studied it. It looked so fragile, but maybe it would hold her if she was very careful. She leant further over, her cold fingers gripping the top of the wooden frame as she gave it a shake to test its strength. It seemed firm enough, so should she take the chance?

For a second which verged on eternity she hesitated, cold fear clamping the muscles in her stomach, then the roar of a curse issuing from the lower regions of the house made her mind up for her. Come what may, she was going down that trellis and now, so help her!

Hands shaking, she dragged off her jacket and tossed it over the side of the balcony, hoping it might cushion her fall if she lost her grip. Then quickly she dragged off her boots and tossed them after it, knowing there was no way she could get a grip on the thin pieces of wood wearing them. She wiped her hands down the sides of her cord jeans, raised her eyes heavenwards in a short, fervent prayer, then cocked her leg over the rail, easing her stockinged toes into the first tiny triangle. She swung her other leg over, clinging to the lip of the balcony with the very tips of her fingers for one heart-stopping moment, then slowly began her descent.

'Where the hell are you?'

The low roar of annoyance came from directly overhead, and Martha froze, flattening herself against the house wall. Chunks of prickly rose bush speared into her chest, stabbing through the layers of thick sweaters, and she caught her breath as she tried to fight against the discomfort. Did he know she was there, or did he think she'd already escaped?

For long minutes she clung to the frame, spreadeagled against the wall, scarcely daring to breathe in case he glanced down. A faint light spilled from the open balcony door, but mercifully she was just a fraction below the outer limits of its beam. If she didn't move, didn't even breathe, then maybe he wouldn't see her.

Minute ran into minute, and Martha could feel her fingers and toes getting colder and stiffer, and knew she couldn't stay there much longer. No matter if he saw her, she would have to move soon or she would fall. Just as she'd reached the very limits of her strength, footsteps crossed the stone floor of the balcony and the light was cut off as the door was slammed with a force which made the whole house shudder. Almost faint from relief, she clung to her precarious perch, then slowly and laboriously made her way down to the ground. Her legs were shaking, trembling from exertion and reaction, and she sat down abruptly on the cold, hard soil, resting her head against her upbent knees. It mightn't have been Everest, but scaling that wall had been for her just as great an achievement!

For a few moments she allowed herself the luxury of just sitting there on the cold but beautifully firm ground, then she forced herself to her feet and scrabbled round in the undergrowth for her jacket and boots. The jacket, draped over a nearby bush, was easy enough to locate, as was one of the boots, but the other just refused to be found. Muttering to herself, Martha crawled on hands and knees across yard after yard of cold, muddy earth, her hands searching squeamishly through the debris of fallen leaves and broken twigs while she tried desperately to find it. It had to be here, not far from the other one, so where on earth could it be?

'Is this what you're looking for?'

The voice was deep and soft, vibrant with amusement, and so shockingly familiar that Martha stopped dead, too stunned to even try and stand up. Slowly she raised her unwilling eyes and stared up at the man who towered over her, one large hand raised aloft, dangling her missing boot from his lean fingers. She swallowed hard, fighting down the bitter, harsh taste of failure. It mightn't be a glass slipper, and he was a million miles away from being Prince Charming, but the outcome was still the same . . . he'd just found the woman he wanted!

'Let me go! You can't keep me here. Let me go, I say!'

She struggled, drumming her stockinged heels as hard as she could against his shins, but apart from a low groan of pain and a tightening of the vice-like grip round her waist he didn't give an inch. Using his shoulder, he pushed the door open and carried her through to the sitting-room, dropping her unceremoniously on to the sofa. Martha gasped as she hit the cushions with a jolt, then rolled to her feet and rounded on him, her green eyes spitting venom.

'If you think you can keep me here like this, then you can think again. I'm going to . . . going to . . .' For a brief, dreadful moment she couldn't think of a single thing to threaten him with, so she just stood and glared at him, like a small cat which had just been cornered by a large and vicious dog, yet refused to give in.

He closed the door, leaning back against the solid wooden panels while he crossed his arms across his broad chest, and just for a moment Martha's attention wavered. Even dressed in worn jeans and thick knit sweater, he was riveting, his dark golden hair gleaming with a burnished sheen, his tanned face like something from a painting. When had she ever seen such a handsome man before? Annoyed at the way her thoughts were wandering, she stood up straighter, pushing the matted dark curls from her hot, flushed cheek, smearing a trail of mud up the side of her face. Her hands were filthy, rims of dirt showing under her nails, the pads of her fingers stained brown with soil. She didn't need a mirror to tell her that she looked a sight, and the knowledge was like a fan to the flames of her anger. He looked like the embodiment of some Greek god and she looked like some filthy, unkempt vagrant. Was there no justice? Hands on hips, she faced him squarely.

'Listen, Mr Maxwell, if you don't let me out of here then I am going to——'

'To what?' he interrupted softly, pushing away from the door to cross the room and stand just inches from her. Instinctively Martha stepped back a pace, intimidated by his height and the solid width of his shoulders. 'Just what are you going to do, Ms Clark? Call the police? Well, there's the phone, so please help yourself. Frankly, I'll be interested to hear what you tell them—what reason you have for coming here tonight.'

His silver eyes were mocking as they stared down at her, and Martha would have given every single thing she possessed, even the much-needed holiday, just to throw the challenge back in his smugly confident face, but she couldn't. She couldn't call the police and explain why she'd come, because, quite apart from the fact that it would be betraying not one but two clients' confidentiality, the police would take a very dim view of how she'd gone about things. The police were rarely in favour of private detective agencies, and never those run by a young and usually attractive woman. There was no way she could risk running foul of them and having her precious licence revoked! In grim, sullen silence she glared her dislike at him, not that it seemed to have much effect on his composure.

'Not going to take me up on the offer, I see. Now I wonder why? Still, we'll leave that till later. Why don't you sit down, make yourself comfortable, and tell me the whole story?'

He crossed the room to pour brandy into two crystal glasses, his back towards her, and for a second Martha stole a glance at the door. Should she make a run for it, try and get to her car? Would she make it? Her legs were still shaky, and he was obviously superbly fit, so did she stand the slimmest chance of escaping?

'Don't forget the deadlock,' he said quietly, without even turning, and she ground her teeth together in annoyance. How had he known what she was thinking? Her eyes fired a hundred thousands darts of hatred at his broad back, but he seemed impervious to them. When he turned, he just smiled at the open hostility on her face and held the glass out towards her. For a second Martha hesitated, loath to accept anything from this wretched man, then common sense made her reach out and take the glass from him. Her knees were still knocking, despite her anger, her insides quivering with both fright and reaction, so maybe she'd be as well to have something to steady her. It might help her to think and find a way out of this whole, dreadful situation . . . if there was one.

She tipped the glass and took a long, deep swallow of the drink, then choked as best ten-year-old brandy hit the back of her throat with all the impact of a karate chop. Tears streamed from her eyes and she gasped, wheezing and coughing as she fought to get air into her lungs. He stepped forwards, catching her firmly by the shoulders, then thumped her hard in the middle of the back, making her lungs whiz open and accept the much-needed air.

'All right?' He still held her, his big hands

warm against her flesh, and Martha nodded before easing herself free from his grasp. Rather abruptly she sat down on the sofa, forcing herself to breathe slowly and evenly in a steady rhythm, keeping her face averted from his too discerning gaze. Surely it had just been the shock of the brandy which had made her feel so unsteady and shaken, not his touch?

He sat down opposite, sipping the amber liquid in his glass with obvious pleasure, while his eyes studied her flushed face, and Martha wriggled uncomfortably in the deep leather seat. She felt like a specimen, something to be studied and viewed under a microscope—and, quite frankly, it wasn't pleasant. She buried her nose in her glass, sipping repeatedly at the drink, feeling the heat curl down into the pit of her stomach in a rather comforting way.

'Would you like another?' He held the bottle up and Martha stared in surprise at her empty glass, then nodded, watching the thin ribbon of liquid pool into the crystal. In the light from the open fire it shone a pale, entrancing golden brown, and she took a quick, appreciative sip, wondering why she'd never realised before just how good brandy was. Why, she was feeling better already.

'Now, then, Ms . . . what on earth is your first name? I can't keep calling you Ms Clark all night, it's quite ridiculous.'

'Why not?' she asked belligerently, then felt her face flush as she realised just how foolish she sounded. What did it matter what he called her: Ms Clark, Spot or Rover? The outcome would be the same whatever.

'It's Martha,' she said shortly, her eyes lifting to study his reaction to this bit of information. He stared at her quietly for a few seconds, his silvery-pale eyes tracing over her small pert features, then he nodded, a faint smile curving his long chiselled lips.

'Yes, it suits you,' he said softly. Just for a moment Martha had the strangest feeling that he'd meant it as a compliment, but why? Why would he want to offer her a compliment when he so obviously disliked her? It was yet another puzzle to add to all the others which were crowding her brain. She drank again, then wriggled deeper into the soft leather chair. So he wanted to ask her some questions, did he? Well, she didn't mind that; frankly, she could handle anything he cared to throw at her. Suddenly Martha was brimful with confidence that she could cope with anything at that moment: run marathons, scale mountains, fight dragons . . . anything, so a few little questions weren't going to bother her. It was all thanks to the restorative powers of this wonderful drink!

'Tell me, Martha, why did you come here tonight?'

He smiled at her, his voice low and softly sensuous, and Martha swallowed, feeling the impact of it ripple through her whole body. She drew in a deep breath while she tried to get her

thoughts into a nice logical order and remember
her story word-perfect, but somehow it was
strangely difficult. A warm, hazy fog seemed to
be drifting through her head, blurring the details
of everything but the truth, and she couldn't tell
him that. No, sirree, she couldn't let the cat out
of the bag!

'I can't tell you.'

For some reason the words sounded funny,
slurred, as though she hadn't said them
correctly—but of course she had. She sat up
straighter and took another swallow of the drink,
a flicker of regret running through her as she
emptied the glass. She picked up the bottle and
poured a scant inch of liquid into her glass,
hating to see it looking so horribly empty. She
took a dainty sip and smiled; that was better.

'Are you sure you can't tell me, Martha?' he
asked quietly. 'You can trust me.'

His face was calm, his voice deeply reassuring,
and for a second Martha was sorely tempted. It
seemed such a pity to have to keep a secret from
him but, after all, she couldn't betray a client.
She shook her head and groaned as the room
began to spin in lazy, colour-filled circles. She
closed her eyes, willing the whirling sensation to
go, but it took quite a while. When she opened
her eyes again he was watching her, his grey eyes
intent, and she had the strangest idea that he
knew just how she'd felt, but of course he
couldn't: he couldn't have known that she would
have such a strange attack of giddiness.

'Well, if you can't tell me exactly why you came, then can you tell me if I'm supposed to know you?'

'Oh, no,' she answered clearly. 'You don't know me, same as I don't know you. That's why I came—well, one of the reasons,' she added as an afterthought, 'to find out your name. What is it?'

'Maxwell,' he said, 'Quinn Maxwell.'

'Thank you,' she said with utmost politeness.

'You're very welcome, but why do you need to know my name?'

'I can't tell you that. It's a secret.' The words twisted themselves into a little knot, then unravelled in a very strange way, but he seemed to understand what she meant.

'Yes, I know it's a secret, honey, but whose secret is it? Yours?'

'Oh, no, course not. Mr Johnson's and Mr . . .'

Her mouth snapped shut as she realised just a fraction too late what she'd done. She looked at him in horror, but there was nothing on his face which even hinted at disapproval. He just smiled at her, and Martha basked in the glow of that smile.

'I don't think I know any Mr Johnson,' he said quietly, a hint of puzzlement in his voice. 'Can you describe him to me?'

Martha thought about that one for a few minutes, resting her chin on the rather dirty heel of her hand. The fire was hissing and spitting softly in the grate, a faint smell of apples coming from the burning logs. Everywhere was so quiet, so beautifully peaceful, not at all like she'd imagined their promised confrontation would be like. Had she been a little bit foolish and hasty to run away like that? Her lids began to droop and she caught herself up, jumping as she felt herself begin to drift into a little sleep. She still had a question to answer, didn't she? What had it been? For a moment her mind struggled through the fog, then she remembered . . . Mr Johnson.

'Mr Johnson is . . . like Mr Johnson,' she said clearly, then giggled at her own cleverness. He grinned, the light from the fire flickering over his handsome face and Martha sighed. He really was the best-looking man she'd ever seen. What a shame he had to be involved in all this.

'What's a shame?'

Martha's heavy lids flicked wide open. She hadn't realised that she'd spoken her thoughts aloud, but she must have. She stared at him, then said slowly, 'You . . . it's a shame that you are involved in all this horrible mess.'

'What mess, Martha? What exactly am I involved in?'

'Can't tell you,' she muttered. 'It's a secret.' She felt so tired, as though everything which had happened had suddenly caught up with her. All she wanted was to put her head down on this nice soft cushion and fall asleep.

'Is it Mr Johnson's secret?' he asked, his voice a bare, soft whisper, and she nodded, too tired to bother with a proper answer.

'Just Mr Johnson's secret?'

'And Mrs Johnson's as well, but I promised I wouldn't tell anyone. My lips are sealed.' She pressed a grimy finger to her lips to emphasise what she'd just said.

'I understand, of course I do. You wouldn't betray a secret, but you can tell me, sweetheart. I won't tell anyone else.'

'Well . . .' She hesitated, her sleepy green eyes lingering on his face.

'Please,' he whispered. He reached out to catch her hand, his long fingers stroking gently over her flesh, and Martha bit down a sudden urge to purr in pleasure. 'You can tell me, Martha; it will be our secret then, yours and mine.'

His voice was gentle, soothing as the wind on a summer night whispering through the trees, and Martha smiled. Surely there could be no harm in telling this gorgeous, handsome man a little secret, not when he was being so kind and understanding? It would be something for them to share, a tiny link which would bond them together.

'You mustn't tell anyone. Promise, cross your heart . . .'

'And hope to die,' he finished for her, his fingers making a cross just above his heart.

'Well, the secret is . . . that you're having an affair with Mr Johnson's wife!'

She hiccuped, then snuggled down into the chair, feeling pleasantly warm and secure. It was good to have someone you could share things with . . . especially secrets!

CHAPTER THREE

MARTHA rolled over, groaning as a dull pain
thudded through her head. She opened her eyes,
then snapped them shut again as the blinding
glare of daylight made them burn. She felt
dreadful. Was she ill? Gingerly she rolled back on
to her stomach, burrowing her face into the
pillow, and sighed in relief at the smooth, cool
touch of silk under her hot cheek. It felt good.

Silk. The word slithered slowly and insistently
into her mind, disturbing the brief moment of
pleasure, though for a few minutes her dulled
brain failed to grasp the reason why. Silk . . . why
should that seem somehow wrong? She lay quite
still, trying to find a way through the clouds of
fog which lingered in her head, and then,
suddenly, she had it. Her bedding was crisp
polycotton, delicately flower-sprigged and
extremely pretty, but it wasn't silk!

Her eyes flew open and she stared at the
smooth, black fabric under her cheek, feeling
suddenly sick. Where was she? Just whose bed
was she in if it wasn't hers? Pressing a hand to
her throbbing temples, she eased herself upright
and stared round the room, her stomach lurching
in shock as she recognised the black and silver

décor at first glance. She was in his room. What was his name, now? That was it, Maxwell, Quinn Maxwell. What in heavens name was she doing in his room, and in his bed?

She leaned weakly back against the soft padded headboard, the implications of the situation too dreadful to contemplate. Somewhere, in the deepest, darkest recesses of her mind, a memory stirred, a fleeting picture of her sitting by a warm, cosy fire sharing a drink with a man . . . that man! After that, it was a total blank. What had happened next? What had she said? Worse still, what had she done? Heaven help her, but she just couldn't remember anything past sitting by that fire. All those hours had passed, and yet she could remember nothing of them!

She flung back the silky covers and half fell out of bed, swaying weakly as pain swamped her head and her knees started to buckle. It was hard to think straight with this terrible pounding in each temple, but she had to try. She had to find a way out of this house before he came in and found her awake. She had the nastiest feeling that she'd already told him more than she should have done, and in this fragile state she would be no match for him if he chose to continue his probing.

'So, you're awake at last. I was beginning to think you would sleep the clock round.'

He came into the room by way of the bathroom, his bare feet making no sound on the thick carpet, and Martha swung round, staggering as her head swirled in protest at the sudden movement. She stared at him, horror shimmering in her green eyes as she studied the short towelling robe he wore. Did he always parade round the house like this, half dressed? Why, she'd seen more of this man's body in just a few short hours than she'd seen of any man in years! She swallowed hard, feeling suddenly far too delicate to handle the situation.

'Your clothes are in the closet,' he said quietly, pointing to the huge walk-in wardrobes which filled one wall of the room.

She nodded, moving instinctively towards them, then froze as the full import of that little piece of information struck her. She glanced down, her eyes lingering in shock for one full second on the pale pink thermal underwear which was all she was dressed in, before she made a leap for the bed. Colour flooded her face and she closed her eyes, wishing she were dead! It just wasn't fair: last night and now . . . this! How could she ever live down the shame of spending the night in this man's bed, and then having him see her clad only in pink long-johns and vest?

The sound of drawers being opened and closed finally made her summon up enough courage to open her eyes, though when she realised what was happening she almost wished she hadn't. For a full minute Martha stared at the broad, golden-tanned back, the smooth curve of naked flanks, the muscled length of his long legs, and felt herself begin to tremble in apprehension.

'What are you doing?' Her voice was a thin

croak, a reedy whistle of cracked sound, but it was the best she could manage right at that moment. Under the covers her hands locked into fists, her short nails digging deep into the soft inner flesh of her palms as she tried to stem the rising tide of panic which threatened to engulf her. If he took one step, just one, towards her, then she would scream the place down, so help her!

'Getting dressed, of course,' he answered, without turning. 'Why? Have you some objection?'

'Yes . . . I mean no . . . I . . . I . . . Why can't you go somewhere else and get dressed?' she managed at last, colour staining her cheeks a brilliant carmine with embarrassment. For a moment there she'd thought he meant to . . . She drew in a shuddery breath, fighting down exactly what she'd thought he intended!

He slid into shorts and jeans before glancing over his shoulder, his silvery-pale eyes unreadable as they studied Martha's flushed face. Then he smiled, a mocking, knowing little smile which made her wish she had something heavy close at hand to throw at him.

'Well, well, so the lady's embarrassed, is she? Now, that is a surprise. I'd have thought you would have seen it all before in your line of business.'

'What do you mean?' Incensed by both the words and the tone in his deep voice, Martha sat bolt upright, clutching the black sheet to her bosom—not that there was the slightest danger of her being immodestly exposed in the thermal outfit. 'What do you mean by my "line of business"? Just what are you implying, Mr Maxwell?'

'Oh, please, call me Quinn. Don't you think that "Mr Maxwell" is just a shade too formal after last night?'

The mockery was open now, but Martha refused to be side-tracked by it, or by that poser he'd just thrown her. There would be time soon enough to find out what had happened last night. Now all she wanted was an explanation of what he'd meant.

'Listen, I don't care what you want to be called. Frankly, I can think up any number of suitable names for you without any help at all. I want to know what you meant by that remark.' She glared at him, pushing the tumbling dark curls from her hot, flushed cheeks with a rough sweep of her hands.

He pulled a soft blue sweater out of a drawer and slipped it on, running his fingers carelessly through his hair to flatten the ruffled golden strands before he answered.

'Nothing much, really, except that I should have imagined that seeing people undressed would be an everyday hazard in your sort of work. After all, aren't divorce cases easier to prove if you catch people *in flagrante delicto*, as the law puts it?'

There was a wealth of scorn in his voice, but

Martha scarcely heard it, too caught up by what
he'd just said. How did he know that she was
working on a divorce case? She'd never told him
that . . . had she? For a moment she tried
desperately to remember their conversation last
night, but it was impossible. That huge great
cloud of fog was still lingering, making it difficult
to remember what day it was, let alone what she'd
said some ten hours previously. But she had to
know how much of what he'd said was based on
fact, and how much on pure guesswork.

'I don't remember mentioning anything about
any divorce case,' she said shortly, her eyes not
quite meeting his.

'Don't you? I suppose it's not surprising,
really, considering the number of brandies you
put away. Now, how many was it? Two . . . three
. . . or was it more?'

His tone was openly mocking, and Martha felt
a sudden surge of shame run through her. How
could she have been so foolish as to do that? She
gritted her teeth and stayed silent, knowing there
was nothing she could say in her own defence.

He moved forwards to stand next to the bed
and stare down at her, and Martha forced down
the sudden urge to slither under the covers and
hide away from his mocking gaze.

'Listen, Ms Clark, you've only got yourself to
blame if you feel lousy this morning. OK, so
maybe I could have tried to stop you drinking so
much. I did think about it at one point, but
frankly I doubted if you would listen to any

advice I had to offer. Anyhow, why should I have bothered? My main concern was to find out what you wanted, not worry about your health and welfare.'

'And did you?' she demanded, embarrassment adding a touch of defiance to her voice.

'Yes, I think I did. Just before you passed out last night, you gave me a clue to what was going on, such a good one that I scarcely needed the rest of the evidence to back it up.'

'What evidence? What are you talking about?' she asked sharply, fear uncurling coldly inside her. What did he know? What had he found?

'This . . . and this.'

With a quick flick he tossed a slim leather wallet and matching notebook on to the silky cover, and for one long second Martha stared at them with wide, disbelieving eyes.

'Recognise them?' he asked softly, his voice just a low purr of sound against the silence in the room. 'I'm sure you must do. After all, I got them out of your pocket.'

It was too much! The final straw after all she'd gone through last night and then this morning. Martha rounded on him in sudden fury.

'How dare you? How dare you go through my things? How dare you invade my privacy like that?'

'Invade *your* privacy?' Naked anger shone in his eyes, and unconsciously Martha shrank back against the headboard, feeling her heart start to pound in sudden terror. He was staring at her with open dislike now, his face hard, his eyes the colour of cold steel, his big hands clenching and unclenching at his sides, as though he was making a tremendous effort to keep them off her. In a flash she knew she had to do something to defuse the situation before it got totally out of control.

'Now, look here, Mr Maxwell—oh!'

The gasp tore from her lips as he leant down and caught her wrist in a harsh grasp, wrenching her forwards so that their faces were bare inches apart.

'No, you look here, Ms Clark. If there was any invasion of privacy last night, it was done by you . . . *you*! Not me.'

'I can explain that, if you'll just let me.'

Desperately she tried to twist free from his grasp, but he just held her tighter, his long fingers locked round the slender bones, making them ache from the pressure. Tears sprang to her eyes, but with an impatient toss of her head she blinked them away. There was no way she was going to give him the satisfaction of making her break down and cry. She stared back at him, her green eyes stormy in her now pale face. For a second he held her gaze, then slowly loosened his hold on her wrist and stepped back a pace, turning his back on her as though he needed a moment to grab hold of his composure. When he spoke, his voice was still harsh, roughened by anger, but more controlled.

'Right, I'm listening. So let's hear it, your

explanation.'

Martha drew in a deep breath, fighting for
some composure of her own before she spoke.
Those last few minutes had near scared her
witless, making her realise just how vulnerable
her position was. But still, if she could just come
up with some sort of plausible explanation, then
maybe she could ease herself out of this dreadful
situation.

'I . . .' Her voice faded and she swallowed hard,
forcing herself to continue. 'As you've already
discovered from the identification in that wallet, I
am a private detective. I came here last night
because I'm working on a case at the moment,
and some information I'd been given led me to
this address. I'm actually trying to locate some
missing property.'

'I see. And what is it exactly that you're looking
for?'

He'd turned back to face her, leaning almost
indolently against the wall, but Martha could tell
from her expression that there was nothing really
indolent about his attention. He was listening to
her every word, listening and weighing up its
merits. Please heaven she could invent something
plausible enough to convince him, because, if she
couldn't, then the consequences might be too
awful to contemplate. In a year filled with sticky
situations, this had to be the stickiest and trickiest
of them all! She cast rapidly round in her mind
for something which would hold the ring of
truth, and came up with the case she'd been

working on only last week.

'Diamonds and pearls. Half a million pounds' worth, to be exact.'

He raised an eyebrow. 'Half a million, eh? Well, well! It appears you work in the big league, then, if you're handling that sort of a case.'

There was a note of disbelief in his voice which Martha just had to quell, right now.

'M.C. Investigations handles many cases of that size. Insurance claims mainly.' There was a note of pride in her voice, but she didn't care who heard it. She'd worked both long and hard to get the company to where it was today, and there was no way she was prepared to dismiss it.

'I am impressed. But how did your investigations lead you here? Surely you don't think that I have half a million's worth of jewels hidden in my cupboards or under the floorboards, do you?'

There was more than a trace of sarcasm in his voice, and Martha flushed, biting her tongue to hold back the hundred or so snappy answers she'd really like to give him. She couldn't afford to do that, to antagonise him further. She had to stay calm, play everything down, and make him think that this whole miserable charade had been one huge mistake from start to finish. If she could do that, then there was just the slimmest chance she would get away with it. M.C. Investigations' whole future could depend on how she played this next scene, so she would have to swallow any insult he cared to throw at her just to protect it.

The business was her lifeblood, her family, her baby . . . and, like any mother, she would do anything in her power to save it from harm!

'Of course I don't think that, Mr Maxwell,' she said with a charming little laugh. 'Why, it's obvious that there's been some sort of a slip-up and that you're not involved.'

'Is it? Why?'

'What do you mean, why?' she snapped, then forced a smile to her stiff lips to soften the abruptness of the question.

'Well, if you believed that I was involved last night, then what has made you change your mind?'

'Well . . . I . . . obviously meeting with you and talking to you has made me realise that you couldn't possibly be involved in anything like that.'

It sounded lame even to her own ears, but Martha refused to dwell on it. There was no way she could afford to let even the tiniest flicker of doubt show on her face, not when he was watching her so intently. She sat up straight, forcing herself to meet his eyes. There was a brief silence, a tiny moment of peace, and then he spoke and that peace was shattered completely.

'Thank you. It's nice to know that what we shared last night obviously influenced your viewpoint. It had a profound effect on me, too.'

His eyes were warm now, no longer hostile, but Martha was too shocked by what he'd said to appreciate it. An icy-cold finger seemed to be stroking down her spine, making her shiver in sudden fear. What did he mean? Just what had they shared that had been so earth-shattering? She licked her suddenly dry lips, desperately wanting to ask the question, yet somehow terrified of hearing the answer.

'You do remember last night, don't you, Martha?' he asked softly, pushing away from the wall to sit down on the side of the bed. 'All of it? Every wonderful moment?'

The mattress dipped under his weight and she slithered helplessly towards him, feeling the tension race through her body as her thigh came to rest against his. Even through the layers of bedding she could feel the hard warmth of his flesh, and desperately she tried to inch herself away. This whole situation was getting way out of hand and she had to do something, but what?

'Oh, surely you're not shy, are you, sweetheart? I don't believe it . . . not after last night.' He reached out, catching her hand gently between both of his to pull her closer, so close that she could smell the faint, tantalising smell of soap and cologne which clung to his skin, feel the sweet, moist warmth of his breath cloud on her cheek. She closed her eyes, fighting for some measure of calm, fighting to make some sense out of this whole crazy situation. Just what should she do, what should she say, faced with this . . . a totally unknown quantity? Last night was like a huge blank canvas, yet even now her imagination was starting to paint some outlines on it: outlines which threatened to blow her mind and destroy her life completely!

She pulled back, managing to set a few precious inches between them before he stopped her, his big hands closing gently but firmly round her slender fingers. She glanced down, staring at her hand, so pale and fragile against his. She could struggle, she supposed, could try to make him free her, yet some instinct warned her that would be a mistake. In a test of strength, there was no doubt as to who would be the winner! No, what she had to rely on now, pin her hopes on, was logic, ice-cold, diamond-bright logic. She'd talked herself out of some tight corners before, so she could do it again.

'Mr M . . .' The words dried up as he bent forwards to gently press one long finger against her lips.

'Quinn,' he ordered softly, staring deep into her eyes, 'please.'

She swallowed hard, trying to ease the huge great knot of tension which threatened to choke her, then tried again.

'All right, then, Quinn. I'm sorry, but I really don't know what is going on here. I don't remember anything about last night.' She tried to keep her voice level, but it wasn't entirely successful.

'Nothing?' He raised one thick eyebrow, a gleam in his eyes which brought a sudden rush of colour to her cheeks and robbed her of any further ability to speak.

'You don't remember me carrying you in here, undressing you, putting you to bed?' His voice was low, sensuous, and Martha bit back a moan of utter misery. Minute by minute, and second by second, everything was getting worse instead of better! Dumbly she shook her head, too distraught to find the right words at that moment.

'None of it? You don't remember lying here in this bed with——'

'Don't!' she cried. 'Please, don't.' She clamped her hands over her ears, desperately trying to cut out his silken voice. She couldn't bear to hear one more word, to have him fill in the detail on all those vivid pictures her mind had just created. If she lived to be a hundred she would never understand how she could have spent the night with this man yet not remember a single thing about it!

She scooted over to the far side of the bed, looking anywhere but at him. If her life had depended on it, she couldn't have done that, not just then. It took an effort to find the strength to speak, but finally Martha managed it. She had to. What was done was done, and though she would regret it till her dying day there was no way to change it. However, equally, there was no way she intended to repeat it!

'Last night . . . well, last night, as you know, I wasn't quite myself. I may have acted in a way which was entirely foreign to me, but I want you to understand that there is no way I shall ever let it happen again.' She looked up, her face stiff with unconscious pride. 'I don't make a habit of sleeping with men I've only just met.'

'I'm glad to hear it,' he said, standing up so that he seemed to tower over her. 'Neither do I make a habit of sleeping with women I've only just met. For your information, I didn't do so last night.'

It took a minute for his words to sink in, like stones dropping into a pool to send out ripples.

'What do you mean?' she asked slowly, staring up at him.

He smiled, a cold, faintly menacing curl of his long lips. 'You're the detective, so you work it out.'

'You mean that I didn't . . . we didn't . . .'

'That's right. We didn't.'

'But why did you let me believe that we . . .?' Colour surged up her pale cheeks and she stopped, too embarrassed and confused to continue with the question.

'Because it was too good an opportunity to miss to pay you back, that's why.'

'Pay me back?' she echoed hollowly, feeling suddenly sick. It had all been a trick, a cruel, distasteful trick.

'Of course. You didn't think you could get away with it, did you? Come here and spy on me, then get away scot-free?'

'Spy on you?' Her head was spinning, whirling with the hangover and a thousand confusing thoughts which refused to be neatly regimented and sorted into any kind of order. The best she could do was to repeat his words.

'Yes. Oh, don't try and act the innocent, there's just no point. One glance at this was all I needed to know what you'd been up to. You've been watching my house for several days now, and this is the proof of it.' He picked up the notebook and tossed it to her, but Martha made no move to catch it. She just watched as it fell to the floor, its white pages fluttering open.

'Dates, times, lists of people coming and going in the street . . . all those sordid little details you specialise in.' His voice was filled with contempt, and she winced, feeling suddenly and strangely ashamed of her actions. But still, if her memory served her right, she'd made no mention of any names in the notebook, nothing but dates and times which could only corroborate her previous story. It was a slim chance, but she had to take it. Anything was better than having to admit the real reason why she had come!

'Look, I've already told you that I am working on a case——' she began, but he interrupted her, his voice hard.

'Yes, you told me all right, and what a pack of lies it was.'

'Lies? How do you know it was lies?' she asked, her tone shrill, bordering on the edges of near-hysteria.

He just looked at her, his face grim, and Martha had to steel herself not to flinch away from that damning look.

'Let me just say one word to you, Ms Clark, just one, a name—and see if it jolts your memory. Johnson. Does it ring a bell? Think on it. I'll be in the kitchen when you've made the connection.'

He left the room, closing the door quietly behind him. Martha stared after him, her eyes wide with a dawning horror. Oh, it rang a bell all right—a great big giant one, and with each peal what she'd said to him last night came clanging back to almost deafen her. She rolled over, dragging the pillow over her head, but it didn't help . . . nothing would. Almost as though she was listening to a tape-recording she could hear herself speaking, saying all those dreadful, indiscreet words, and she groaned aloud in dismay.

'You're having an affair with Mr Johnson's wife!'

Time and time again they echoed round her head, becoming ever more dreadful by the second. How could she have said them? How? Because he'd tricked her.

The answer slid into her mind and she flung the pillow as hard as she could across the room, knowing it was right. She, who had always considered herself streetwise and smart, had been outsmarted by that . . . that Lothario!

She washed and dressed in record time, then made her way to the kitchen, pausing just a step inside the doorway. Quinn Maxwell was seated at the table, reading, a pale wintry sun filtering through the small-paned window, bouncing flashes of golden fire from his downbent head and setting his dark-tanned face in shadow. For a moment Martha felt her stomach tighten, then roll with a sudden attack of the jitters.

Just who was he? Who was this man who'd just turned her neat and ordered life upside-down, then twisted it on its axis? This case should have been pure routine, a well-rehearsed sequence of dates and times and numbers, yet this man had destroyed any hope of that completely.

He glanced up, his eyes part shadowed from where he sat with his back to the window, and Martha wished desperately that she could have seen the expression in their depths. It would, at least, have given her a clue on how to play the next few minutes, because that was something she needed. Never had she been in such an intolerable position before, never!

There was silence for a few long seconds, a silence which stretched her nerves and patience to their limits, then he lifted the glass coffee-pot and poured a mugful of the dark brew, pushing it across the table towards her.

'Here, drink this. You look as though you need it.'

It was hardly the most hospitable of offers to a guest, even an uninvited one as she was, but Martha supposed that it was better than that strained, disturbing silence. She sat down, cradling the mug in her hands while she sipped the coffee, and shuddered at the bitter taste. It was dreadful!

'Have you any sugar?' she asked, knowing she would never be able to drink it like this, no matter how much she needed the boost it would give her.

'In the cupboard over the fridge, I think,' he answered, without looking up from his paper. It was the *Financial Times*, she noted, standing up to search through the cupboard; a strange choice for a man like him. She hunted round till she found a crumpled bag of sugar right at the back of the deep cupboard, and carried it back to the table, poking at the solid crystals till she had enough free for a couple of spoonfuls. She ladled it into the drink, then stirred it briskly, praying it would take the edge off this witches' brew he called coffee.

'Well, have you remembered, then?' He folded the paper and laid it down next to his mug, and Martha felt her stomach perform a neat little somersault, complete with double tuck. It was obvious that he expected answers now, yet just what could she tell him? Granted, he'd already sussed out the real reason why she'd arrived on his doorstep, but how could she tell him the full story and betray her client's confidence? It was so unethical, so far against every principle she'd held dear since starting the company. Deep down she knew that she would almost prefer to face the rack, and a thousand other tortures, than do that with any degree of willingness. She took a long swallow of the hot liquid, feeling it scorch the back of her throat, hoping it would help her think.

'Well?'

She set the mug down, her hand lingering against its smooth, earthenware surface, needing something to cling to, something solid in a world which seemed to be slipping through her fingers.

'Yes.' Her voice was low and she cleared her throat, hating to hear the note of indecision, hating him to know just how disturbed she was by having to make the confession. 'Yes. I remember exactly what I said last night.'

'And do you think it warrants an explanation?' His face was set, his eyes grim as they studied her, and Martha held his gaze with an effort. In truth she could appreciate why he was angry, but it just wasn't her concern. Her main concern now must be to protect her client.

'I don't think that there's any explanation needed. You know the facts. You're quite right in your assumption of why I came, and that, as far as I can see, is the end of it.'

'You're a cool one, I'll say that for you, Martha Clark—a real cool customer. But I'm afraid that isn't the end of it.'

'No?' She raised one slender eyebrow, her face holding just the smallest trace of mockery. 'Well, I'm afraid that's all I'm prepared to tell you, so I don't really see how you can make any more out of it.'

'Don't you, indeed?' His voice was low, almost

menacing, and Martha felt a ripple of fear tingle up her backbone. Somehow, she had the strangest feeling that his words held more than just a hint of threat. She looked down at the dark liquid in the cup, tilting it from side to side so that a tiny whirlpool formed on its glassy surface. She had the nastiest feeling that his thoughts were like this: dark, bitter and, to her at least, totally unpalatable! She had to get out of the house fast before she really got a taste of what was lurking under the surface of his mind.

'Mr Maxwell, last night I came here following up on a case—and through one thing and another, things got completely out of hand. Now all I want to do is leave and forget that any of it ever happened.'

'I'm sure you do, but I'm afraid it's just not that simple. I object to you coming here spying on me, Ms Clark. I object to you monitoring my friendships and my life just because you find it an easy way to make a living.'

Easy? That was a laugh. So far she'd been terrorised, pursued and drunk herself into a stupor, and he called it an easy way to make a living! A hundred replies surged to Martha's lips, but she snapped them closed, refusing to give life to any one of them. If she started that, then there was no chance he would ever let her go this side of Doomsday! No, if she had to placate him to get out of the house, then she would do so, even if it choked her.

'This isn't getting us anywhere, now, is it?

Look, what's done is done, so where's the point in going back over old ground? I really think it would be better for both of us if I leave now.'

She pushed back her chair and walked briskly from the kitchen, her heart hammering hard in her throat as she heard the sound of his footsteps following.

'Just a minute. Before you go, I want your assurance that this whole business is going to end here.'

'What do you mean?' She turned to face him and stepped back a pace, not realising that he'd come up so close behind her. In the narrow hall he seemed to tower over her, his wide shoulders blotting out the faint light which spilled from the kitchen doorway. All of a sudden Martha felt strangely breathless as the memory of what had so nearly happened last night at this very spot came back to assail her. Just for a moment she could almost feel the warmth of his breath as it touched her skin, feel the hard, muscled strength of his chest under her palms once again. She glanced down, terrified of what he might read in her face. She might dislike this man, might feel nothing but contempt for what he was doing, yet he still had a strange ability to disturb her. It had been years since she'd felt so shaken by a man's closeness, years since she'd felt this rush of physical awareness.

'I want you to promise that you will give up this case.'

His voice was low, slightly rough, and just for a

moment she wondered if he, too, was having trouble with the same disturbing memories. But that was foolish. To a man like Quinn Maxwell, that brief moment must mean less than nothing.

She took a slow, deep breath, trying to ease the lingering echoes from her mind so that she could deal with the present.

How could she promise to give up the case when she had already made a commitment to her client, or rather, clients? After all, this wasn't just one case but two: Mr Johnson and Mr Morris. There was really no way she could do it, yet she had the unnerving feeling that he would never let her go unless she gave her word. She'd already sneaked a look at the door, and the key was still missing, so, unless she agreed, then she could find herself locked in this house for just as long as it pleased him. Suddenly the thought of being closeted in his company for much longer was more than Martha could bear. She cast round, desperate for some sort of solution, and came up with the perfect answer.

She could promise to give up the case, and *she* would stick to that promise, but that didn't mean that she couldn't hand it over to someone else, one of the men who worked for her. She'd been thinking about doing that yesterday before this whole crazy charade started, so she might as well decide to do it. She looked up, her green eyes clear and level as they met his intent grey ones.

'I promise that I will have no further part in

watching you or your house,' she said, choosing her words with care.

He stared at her in silence for a few minutes, studying her face, and Martha forced herself not to flinch. Then he smiled, a slow, sensuous smile which made her pulse leap up and start to flutter in a wild, crazy little rhythm she couldn't control.

'Thank you,' he said softly. 'I'm sure you won't regret it. Next time we meet, then at least this won't be lying between us.'

Next time? No way was there ever going to be a next time if she could help it. It would be far too dangerous, both for her business and, more importantly, herself!

'I hardly think there will be a next time,' she said weakly, edging towards the door.

'Don't you? I disagree. I think fate led you here last night, and that same fate will have some bearing on the future. But still, only time will tell, won't it?'

He reached past her to unlock the door, and Martha turned to hurry through it, stopping dead as she found herself face to face with a woman standing on the step. She gasped in surprise and stepped back a pace, backing into the solid length of the man who was behind her. Instinctively his hands closed round her shoulders to steady her, and Martha felt her breath catch at the feel of his warm, firm grasp.

'Oh, I'm sorry. Did I startle you? I was just about to knock.'

She stepped into the hall, smiling at Martha

before turning to Quinn.

'I hope I'm not too early, Quinn, dear, but I thought we could make an early start today as I have a WI meeting after lunch. I can come back later if you're busy, though.'

'No, not at all, Margaret,' he said easily, letting his hands slide from Martha's shoulders and down the length of her arms in a light touch which burned a trail of fire down her flesh. 'Martha is just leaving, so I have plenty of time.' He smiled at the older woman, his grey eyes warmer than Martha had ever seen them. 'Allow me to introduce you two ladies—Margaret Johnson, I'd like you to meet Martha Clark.'

He stepped back, and Martha stared round her in something verging on panic. This couldn't be happening, it just couldn't. To come face to face with the woman here—why it was like the darkest point in some dreadful nightmare!

'I'm pleased to meet you, Miss Clark.' Mrs Johnson held out her hand and Martha was forced to take it. 'Why, your hands are like ice, dear! Surely you're not going out without a coat on? You'll catch your death on a bitter day like this.'

'I . . . I . . .' Martha stuttered and stammered, then found her voice, though it sounded as though it belonged to someone else. 'I must have left my coat somewhere,' she said lamely, looking round.

'It's in the bedroom. I'll get it.'

He walked unhurriedly down the hall, and for a

second Martha stared after him, feeling desperate. Pure common courtesy demanded that she should say something, make some attempt at conversation, but what? However, the ball was taken out of her court as the older woman spoke.

'Have you known Quinn long?' There was a note of speculation in her voice, and in a trice Martha realised what could have caused it. She flushed, the colour surging under her pale, fine skin as she acknowledged just how damning it looked to have left her coat in his bedroom.

'Oh, no. No, we only just met last night,' she said quickly to put the record straight, then realised that was even worse than saying nothing! 'I mean, I . . .'

The older woman laid her hand gently on Martha's arm, her face filled with understanding. 'I know exactly what you mean, my dear, and I can't blame you. He's quite a man, isn't he? So handsome and so charming. He could sweep any girl off her feet.'

Well, maybe the description wasn't quite what Martha would have chosen for him, or at least a major part of it. He was handsome, all right, almost too handsome, but charming? She'd not had a single taste of that, had she? Unable to agree or disagree, she merely smiled, wishing he would hurry up finding her jacket. It seemed to be taking him an inordinately long time.

'Yes, my life has certainly changed since I met

Quinn, Miss Clark, become fuller, richer. I feel years younger, in fact. I must say it's been worth every penny, every single penny.'

The words filtered through her embarrassment, though for a moment Martha failed to grasp the full implication of them. Then suddenly it hit her, just what the woman had said, every single revealing word of it. She turned round, her eyes wide with a dawning horror.

'You pay him, pay him for his . . . services?' Her voice was shrill, echoing down the narrow hallway like a whistle through a tunnel, and she winced, glancing quickly along the hall, wondering if he'd heard her. However, there was still no sign of him returning with her coat.

'But of course I do, dear. Why, we all do. After all, it's the way he makes his living, and he is so very good at it.'

Mrs Johnson smiled at her, a gentle, faintly amused little smile, but Martha wasn't looking at her now. She was staring past her, her eyes locked on the tall figure walking down the hall. She felt numb, shocked to the core, rigid with a horror so great that her brain was finding it hard to function. Yet one word was trying to ease its way through the shock, to wriggle into her consciousness, a word so old, so scarcely used, that it conjured up immediate pictures of tents and harems and dark-eyed men like Valentino. She stared at Quinn Maxwell as he came closer, stared and stared and couldn't take her eyes from him, the 1980s version of a kept man . . . a gigolo. A professional lover!

CHAPTER FOUR

IT HAD been a long day. Martha swallowed the last of the hot milk, then left the cup on the table, too tired to even make the effort to wash it. Though it was barely ten o'clock, all she wanted to do now was to get to bed and put the whole of this miserable day behind her. As days went, this could win an award for the worst one ever!

She switched off the living-room light, then made her way wearily through to the bedroom, her eyes going automatically to the framed photograph on the bedside-table. She picked it up and stared down at it, her fingers smoothing gently over the cold, hard glass, tracing the familiar features.

It had been taken almost ten years ago now, when Paul had been twenty, and he looked so young, younger even than she remembered him. What would he have looked like now? How would the years have changed him? Hugging the photo to her, Martha tried to imagine how his face might have changed, how the years could have altered all those youthful contours. She closed her eyes, concentrating on putting flesh and substance back on to the flat paper image, but it was impossible: impossible to take the past

74

and turn it into the present.

Paul had been dead three years now, and no amount of wishing could change that fact. She should be grateful that she had her photographs and all those precious memories of the wonderful years they'd been married. It was more than most people had in a whole lifetime.

With a tiny sigh she put the photograph back and unbuttoned her dressing-gown, tossing it carelessly at the bottom of the bed before sliding between the cool crisp sheets with a soft murmur of relief. It was good to be in her own bed, to have all her own familiar things around her. It made her feel safe, secure, as though she was in charge of her life once more. What had happened last night and then this morning had shaken her more than she cared to admit. It was only now, hours later, that she felt truly able to cope with it.

That man, and what she'd discovered about him, had disturbed her greatly, but now she had to put the whole unsavoury incident behind her. She'd already taken the first step towards doing that by handing the case over to one of her employees. So now Quinn Maxwell and all his women were no longer her immediate concern. She would keep overall control of the case, as she did with every case the agency handled, but it was no longer one of her priorities—and that was a relief. The less she had to do with that man and his unprincipled life-style, the better!

She switched off the lamp and rolled over,

pulling the covers snugly round her shoulders, but the sleep which had been so welcoming just minutes earlier now proved to be elusive. She tossed and turned, rolling restlessly round the bed, wondering why she'd never realised before just how lumpy the mattress really was. The trouble was that, although her body was tired, her brain was still annoyingly active. Maybe she should read for a while and see if that would settle her down.

She sat up and reached for the light switch, gasping in alarm as the telephone suddenly rang, its strident tones almost deafening in the silence. She snatched up the receiver to cut off the dreadful racket, wondering who on earth could be calling at this hour.

'Hello?'

'Ms Clark . . . it's George.'

'George?' For a full second Martha stared at the phone in utter confusion. George Bryant was one of her employees, but what did he want, ringing her at this hour?

'Are you still there, Ms Clark?'

'Yes, of course, George. What is it? Has something happened?'

'It's that case you gave me today. Well, I've been keeping tabs on that Maxwell chap, as you told me to—not that it's been easy, mind you. He's led me a right merry dance, I can tell you. But now, well, now . . .'

His voice trailed off and Martha felt the back of her neck start to prickle in sudden swift apprehension. George was one of her best men, an ex-police officer who'd proved time and again that he could handle any sort of situation. It was the main reason she'd put him on this case, knowing he would be equal to anything Quinn Maxwell could come up with. So what had happened to instil that note of worry in his voice?

She took a slow, deep breath, willing herself to stay calm and prepare herself for any sort of· eventuality. Maxwell had been trouble from the word go, and from the look of things had every intention of continuing to be so, but she had to deal with him the same as she'd dealt with so many others.

'Just tell me what's happened, George,' she said firmly, pleased to hear just how calm she sounded, though inside every nerve in her body felt as though it was twanging. 'Is there some sort of a problem with the case? It seemed quite straightforward to me, just a simple surveillance. Come to think about it, what are you doing working at this time? I thought I explained that he wasn't down for twenty-four hour surveillance, and that you could finish around eight.'

'I know that, Ms Clark, but around a quarter-to he took off, so I figured I'd better follow and see what he was up to.'

'So what happened? Did you lose him?' Annoyance echoed briefly in her voice at that idea, but the man was quick to reassure her.

'No way, though it's been touch and go a few

times, I can tell you. We must have driven a couple of hundred miles around town tonight, just going up and down back streets, but I'm still with him. It's just that . . . hold on, will you? I'm in a pay phone and I'm going to run out of money.'

Martha chewed on her lip, forcing herself to wait patiently while he fed more coins into the slot.

'Sorry about that, Ms Clark.'

'That's OK, George, but go on. You say you're still with him, so what's the problem? Where exactly are you?'

There was a brief, tense silence, and Martha had the strangest feeling that the man didn't know how to answer the simple question.

'George!' she snapped out, suddenly losing patience.

'Outside your flat.'

'Outside my . . . what on earth do you mean?' she demanded in astonishment.

'Just that. We drove round and round as I told you, going in circles most of the time, then he took off and drove like a madman right across town. I couldn't believe it when he pulled up outside your door. I've no idea what's going on, maybe you have, but I thought I'd better warn you.'

'You did quite right, George, thank you. Where are you phoning from?'

'The box on the corner. What do you want me to do now? Wait and see where he goes next?'

'No,' she said slowly. 'No, you go on home. I'll handle this myself.'

Martha replaced the receiver, then sat quite still, trying to absorb this new piece of information and make some sense of Quinn Maxwell's actions. Just what did he want? It couldn't be coincidence that his night-time drive had led him there.

She slid out of bed, dragging on her robe as she walked quickly through to the living-room and eased the curtains open just a fraction. The window overlooked the front street, and for a few minutes Martha stared down, her eyes lingering on the half-dozen or so cars parked along the kerb. Which one was his? She couldn't tell from this distance.

Lower down the street a car pulled out and drove slowly past, and she frowned as she realised it was George's. Obviously he was following her instructions and going home, so now it seemed it really was down to her to sort the whole crazy situation out.

She ran back to the bedroom and dragged on jeans and sweater over her nightgown, tucking the silky folds inside with scant regard for the oddly bundled shape they made of her slim figure. What she looked like was of no importance now, when she had this other pressing problem to deal with. All she wanted was to sort it out, and get rid of that man as fast as possible. It made her feel strangely vulnerable to think of him parked outside her home.

She let herself out of the flat and ran down the stairs to street level, opening the front door quietly to peer out. The road was quiet at this hour and she hesitated for a few seconds, somehow loath to leave the safety of the doorway. Then, chiding herself for being foolish, she stepped out and walked briskly along the pavement, checking each of the cars in turn.

He was in the third one, a long silvery saloon which must have cost a small fortune from the look of its sleek lines. Martha stopped dead when she came level with it, her green eyes shooting sparks as they met his mocking grey ones through the tinted windscreen. She pounded on the side door, waiting with a mounting fury while he pressed a button and the window slid down a couple of inches. A blast of warm air seeped out of the car and she shivered, wishing she'd stopped long enough to find a jacket before she'd rushed out. However, mere cold was the very least of her worries.

'What the hell do you think you're doing?' she demanded hotly.

He smiled at her, his eyes gleaming as he noted the fury on her face. 'What does it look like?'

'It looks like you're sitting outside my home, causing a nuisance,' she snapped back.

'Does it?' he replied easily, not a trace of discomfort on his face.

'But why? Why are you here at this time of the night?'

'Oh, just testing out a theory.'

'Theory . . . what theory? What are you talking about?'

'My, my, you are in a temper. Does it bother you so much, the fact that I'm here?' There was a note of speculation in his deep voice which made Martha flush when she heard it.

'Of course it bothers me. It would bother me no matter who it was out here, not just because it's you! Exactly what right have you to be here?'

'Same right as you have to be outside my house, I imagine,' he answered, his voice suddenly hard.

His meaning was unmistakable and Martha stepped back a pace, wondering what to do next. She cast a frantic look up and down the street, wrapping her arms tightly round her body as the icy wind knifed through her sweater. Just what could she do to make him go away? She would never be able to rest, knowing he was out here.

'Here, get in before you catch your death.' There was concern in his voice now as he swung the car door open, but she hesitated, somehow loath to entrust herself to him in that small, confining space.

'Well, please yourself. It'll be your funeral.' He leant over to close the door, but she wrenched it back and slid inside, trying hard not to shiver as a delicious warmth spread through her numb body. She tucked her hands under her arms and clamped her teeth together to stop them chattering, then stared at him, determined not to let him see just how much he disturbed her.

He was wearing a thick leather flying-jacket, the collar pulled high around his well-shaped ears, and in the dim light from the dashboard his hair was like rich old gold, his eyes like burnished pewter. For a few minutes Martha studied him in silence, feeling a ripple of regret course through her that behind all this male beauty should lie such a devious and treacherous nature.

'Well,' he said softly, 'are you going to sit there all night and stare at me, or are you going to ask me what I want?'

Martha's face tightened as she heard the sarcasm in his voice, her full lips compressing into a flat line.

'So, what do you want?' she snapped at him.

'So gracious,' he said with a mocking little laugh. 'Your manners, my dear Ms Clark, leave me speechless.'

'Let's forget my manners, shall we? Yours are nothing to write home to Mother about, believe me. What exactly do you want? What is this "theory" you mentioned?' She half turned in the seat to face him, the dim light playing gently over her fine pale skin, so that for a moment she looked far younger than her thirty years. He looked at her in silence for a few seconds, and Martha found to her surprise that she couldn't think of one single sharp and scratchy thing to say to make him look away. Why was he watching her like that, staring at her as though he found the experience pleasant?

She squashed down the urge to run her fingers

through her untidy curls to make herself look less dishevelled. It was just tactics, that was all, a trick to make her believe he found her attractive and thereby soften her up, but it wouldn't work. She was no poor, lonely, middle-aged woman, unsure of herself and worrying over her waning youth. She was her own person, a capable, determined businesswoman, who had stood on her own two feet for years!

'Look, Mr Maxwell, you can just cut out all those smouldering looks. They don't work on me. I'm immune to you and your brand of charm.'

'Are you? I don't suppose you'd care to test that out, would you?'

He moved closer and Martha stifled a gasp as she huddled up against the door. She scrabbled round for the door-handle, but despite her efforts the door refused to open.

'Central locking system,' he said briefly, an amused glitter in his eyes. 'There's no way you can get out until I let you . . . yet again.'

'Now, look here——' she began hotly, anger flaring inside her that she had fallen for the same old trick once again. He held his hand up, his face suddenly hard as he interrupted.

'No. You look here, Ms Clark. This morning you promised that you would drop the case, yet what do I find this afternoon? Only that there is one of your men parked outside my house!'

'How can you be sure of that?' she asked quickly. 'It could have been anyone. After all, I'm sure there's quite a few irate husbands dying to know what their wives are up to. So why do you think he was one of my men?'

He grinned, a taunting curve to his long lips which sent a shiver of unease tingling down her backbone. 'Because you're here.'

'Pardon?' she said, puzzled at such an ambiguous answer.

'Surely it's obvious? Look, I spotted this man around six o'clock but decided to give him the benefit of the doubt in case I was getting paranoid after last night. However, when he was still there at seven-thirty, then I knew that my suspicions must be right. So I took him for a little drive, then made my way here. I figured that if he really was one of your men, then he would waste no time in contacting you. So . . . here you are, and it seems that my theory was right.'

He sat back in his seat, a smugly complacent look on his face which made Martha itch to reach out and smack him. He made it all sound so easy, absolute child's play, yet she knew for a fact that George was *the* best when it came to surveillance work. Quinn Maxwell must be far sharper than she'd allowed for; she would have to watch out. Mind you, was it any surprise that he'd developed his instincts for self-preservation? In his line of business, it was a basic necessity! Playing for time, a few precious minutes to work out what to do next, she said shortly, 'And how did you know where I live?'

He shrugged, his big shoulders moving briefly under the thick leather jacket, brushing against hers in the confined space.

'I checked your licence last night. I had a feeling I might need to know a bit more about you, and it seems I was right.'

How could she have been so careless? Martha made a mental note to never carry such revealing information next time she was out on a case. There was no way she wanted her address being disclosed like this, handed out to any Tom, Dick or Harry. In some cases it could prove to be very dangerous; it had proved to be—well, rather hazardous in this one. She looked up, her green eyes steady as they met his across the few inches which separated them.

'So, it seems you've caught me out. What happens next?'

'That depends on you.'

'In what way?'

'All you have to do is call off your hounds, then we can either go our separate ways . . . or let our relationship develop along friendlier lines. I know which I'd prefer.'

There was no mistaking what he meant, and Martha flushed, filled with a fresh surge of temper.

'*We* don't have a relationship and, as far as I'm concerned, shall never have one. I despise everything you stand for, Quinn Maxwell. Despise the way you prey on silly, vulnerable women in this manner. This car, for instance, it must have cost a packet. Which one of your lady friends paid for it?'

'Which one of my . . .? Just what do you think I do for a living? Tell me!'

'I should have thought that was obvious,' she snapped back, annoyed that he should pretend such innocence.

'Oh, it is, but just let me get it straight and check the facts. You not only believe that I have affairs with married women, but that I live off them, do you?' His face had tightened, turning into a mask of anger, so that for a moment Martha half regretted stating her views so plainly.

'Well——'

'Listen, lady, I earned this car, for your information. Earned every penny it took to buy it.'

'How?' she snapped back, suddenly too incensed to be cautious. 'By taking those poor women to your b . . . oh!' Her head snapped back on her slender neck as he jerked her forwards, his long fingers locked round a clump of her sweater.

'You have a very nasty mind, d'you know that, Martha Clark? A very nasty, evil mind. How I earn my money is between me and my clients, no one else. I might explain it to you some day, but don't hold your breath!'

She pulled back, fighting to break free, but he wouldn't let her go. She rounded on him, furious at her own helplessness.

'I don't want to hear any explanations you can ever give me. I know what you do for a living; Mrs Johnson was quite clear about it this morning. I just don't know how you can live with yourself!'

Her voice was harsh, and just for a moment a trace of indecision crossed his face. She had the sudden strange feeling that he wanted to tell her something important, but she didn't want to hear. She twisted round, wrenching the soft wool of her sweater out of his fingers.

'Will you please open the door?'

'Certainly, when you promise to call off your men. Oh, I appreciate the tactics you've employed: you promised to give up the case and I suppose that you, personally, have done so, but there's no way I'm going to put up with being watched day and night by someone else.'

'No? So what are you going to do about it?' she asked defiantly, loath to give an inch. 'Abduct me, sell me to white slave traders, or just keep me locked up in this car for the next ten years?' She glared at him, a mutinous set to her face. There was a moment's silence, then he seemed to come to a decision.

'No, I suppose that would be unrealistic, wouldn't it? No matter how tempting a few of those options seem. I suppose I shall have to let you go and try to find some other way to convince you that what you're doing is wrong. Actually, I have the idea it could be quite enjoyable, really.' He flicked a switch and the door clicked open. Martha opened it wide and shivered as a blast of wintry air flowed over her skin. She stared at him, desperately wanting to know what he meant by that last little comment. In the dim half-light his face was shadowed, his eyes unreadable, and she knew the only way to find out would be to ask him, but she wouldn't do that, not even to save her life! It would sound like she was admitting defeat.

She turned to get out, then stopped abruptly as he caught her hand in a firm yet strangely gentle clasp. She turned back, ready to tell him in no uncertain terms to let her go, but fell silent as he lifted her hand, drawing her fingers gently down the side of his lean cheek. Martha was barely able to stifle a gasp at the unexpected contact with his warm, firm flesh. Holding her gaze, he drew the tips of her fingers slowly over all the hard planes and carved angles of his face, stopping just a hair's breadth away from his chiselled lips.

'Flesh and blood, Martha, feel it. I'm just a human being, and I'm willing to admit it, but are you?'

'What do you mean?' she stammered, almost speechless from shock and another emotion she refused to dwell on.

'Just that you obviously believe that you are incapable of making a mistake. But one day you will have to face the fact that you can't always be right, that even you can look at the evidence yet draw the wrong conclusions. Think about it, Martha. Really think about it, before it's too late.'

He let her go and Martha climbed from the car, her legs unsteady. She hurried inside, leaning back against the door while she tried to find enough strength to climb the stairs. In the distance she could hear the throbbing note of his car as he drove away, a pulsing echo of sound almost as loud as her rapid heartbeat.

Was he right? Had she made some sort of a mistake, taken the facts and then evaluated them the wrong way? She couldn't see that she had, but the first tiny seed of doubt had been sown to disturb her for the rest of the night.

CHAPTER FIVE

A HEAVY, noisy pounding on the front door woke Martha from sleep, a sleep which had been laced with dreams and shadows she didn't want to remember. She pulled herself upright, shaking her head to chase the lingering echoes of it away. A face had kept appearing in those dreams, a hard, tanned face with silvery eyes and a mocking smile, and she desperately tried to erase the memory of it from her mind. For a brief second she stared at the photograph, feeling strangely guilty that another man should have intruded on her dreams in that way. It had never happened before, not once in all these years.

She almost fell out of bed, her head spinning at the abrupt awakening, and struggled to the front door, clutching the robe tightly round her shoulders.

'Who is it?' she managed to croak through sleep-parched lips.

'Delivery for Ms Martha Clark.'

At this hour? Why, it was barely . . . Martha gasped as she caught sight of the clock, biting back a groan as she realised that she'd overslept and would be late for work yet again! Twice in as many days was getting beyond a joke!

Galvanised into action by the discovery, she wrenched the door open, her eyes widening as she spotted the long, golden florist's box the boy was holding.

'Ms Clark? Sign here, please.'

He thrust the box and a small slip of paper into her hands, and Martha hastily scrawled her signature, too stunned to even think of refusing. It had been ages since she'd been sent flowers; who could be sending them to her now? The boy turned to go, and suddenly she found her voice.

'Wait! Who are they from?'

He grinned at her. 'Dunno, miss. I only make the deliveries. There's probably a card inside. See you.'

Whistling softly, he walked off down the hallway, and slowly Martha closed the door and carried the box inside. She pulled off the lid, staring down in disbelief at the sheaf of pale yellow roses nestling in the folds of crackling waxed paper. There must have been three dozen perfect long-stemmed blooms in the box, which would have cost a fortune at this time of the year. Who on earth could have been rash enough to send them?

She set the box carefully down on the table while she searched through the folds of paper for a card, a message, something to tell her who had sent this exquisite present, but there was nothing and she felt more perplexed than ever. Just who would go to the trouble of sending her flowers, yet not even send a message?

Puzzling over who it could be, Martha went into the kitchen and filled a vase with water, breathing in the heady, delicious perfume of the roses. Once they were arranged to her liking, she carried them back into the living-room and set them on a side table where they made a glowing patch of colour against the plain white walls.

For a few minutes she studied them, noticing how they seemed to bring the room to life, to give it character and a sense of being lived in. It was hard to believe that she'd lived in this flat almost two years now, yet had left so little sign of her presence. Everywhere was neat and clean, the rooms all tastefully furnished, yet for some reason the flat seemed to lack that certain something which stamped it with the hallmark of its owner. It was her home, yet Martha knew it held little place as such in her heart. She could leave here tomorrow without a backward glance or twinge of sadness. It was just somewhere to live, to eat a meal and sleep for however many hours, but beyond that it meant nothing to her. Her office had more character than this place: she had put more of herself into those rooms than into these, which were meant to be her home. The sudden realisation disturbed her.

Jeannie was hard at work by the time she arrived at the office, and Martha felt her face fill with colour as she saw the look of speculation on the girl's face at her late arrival. She hurried through to her room and closed the door firmly behind her, needing a few quiet moments to regather her composure. Being late not just once but twice was unsettling, breaking the neat and orderly pattern of her existence. Her life had always been so strictly arranged, timetabled and mapped out to the very last second, and there was no way she wanted that to change, no way she wanted to leave room in her life for feelings or emotion. She'd already run the whole gamut of emotions, had hit the depths of pain and despair after knowing the dizzy heights of happiness, and now all she wanted was to stay somewhere in the middle and never touch those two extremes again. She didn't think she could survive that sort of emotional upheaval once more.

Determined to put all the unsettling thoughts to the back of her mind, she settled down and tried to work, but for some reason she couldn't seem to get a grip on what she was doing. So much seemed to be whirling round in her head, so many strange, disturbing ideas, and most of them centred on that damnable Quinn Maxwell! The sooner she finished with the case, the better she would like it, but for now she must try to find some way to get him out of her head.

She opened a new file and read carefully through the details, making notes as various points struck her. It promised to be an interesting case, a possible fraud involving several valuable paintings, and gradually Martha became engrossed in the complexities of it. There was just something about it which didn't quite add up, if she could only put her finger on it. She turned back to the beginning of the file and re-read the first few pages, seeking the elusive little clue her subconscious had spotted but her mind kept missing.

The telephone buzzed softly by her elbow, and she slowly picked up the receiver, her mind still busy. Why hadn't the guard reported the loss sooner? Why had there been a time lapse of almost twenty minutes . . .?

'Martha? Is that you sitting so silently at the other end of this line?'

The low, amused voice got her attention all right, all of it! She jumped violently, scattering papers from the desk to the floor, where they lay fanned across the carpet. Heart pounding, she jammed the receiver tighter against her ear, praying she'd been mistaken in identifying the caller, but of course she hadn't.

'Martha . . . surely you're going to answer me, sweetheart? You're not sulking about last night, are you?'

'Don't "sweetheart" me, Quinn Maxwell. What do you want?' She drew in a deep breath, flattening her hand over the mouthpiece so he couldn't hear any telltale noises and realise just how much his unexpected call had startled her.

'Now, is that any way to speak to me after I sent you all those beautiful flowers? I had hoped they would put you in a better frame of mind.'

He had sent the flowers? For a few dizzy moments Martha felt her head reel at the thought, before deliberately forcing herself to calmness. She couldn't let the shock of the revelation throw her completely off balance. It was probably exactly what he'd hoped for.

'It would take more than a few flowers to make me feel softer towards you, Mr Maxwell. So, let me repeat, what exactly do you want now? I thought we'd said all there was to be said last night.'

There was a sudden brief silence, and she had the strangest feeling that he was weighing up how best to continue, but there was no way she was going to give him that sort of advantage. With an opponent of Quinn Maxwell's calibre, one had to punch first and hardest!

'Look, I'm very busy, so if you've just rung to make a nuisance of yourself yet again, then forget it. Goodbye.'

Briskly she lowered the receiver towards its cradle, halting reluctantly as he said swiftly, 'Wait! Can't you even spare me a couple of minutes?'

Martha glanced at her watch, checking the second hand before replying crisply, 'Two minutes, no more, no less, then I hang up.'

'OK, I suppose I'll have to take it if it's the best you can offer. I sent you those flowers partly as an apology for disturbing you last night, and partly in the hope that they would soften your rather hard-nosed attitude towards me. We need to talk, Martha, to really get down to the basics and work out some sort of sensible compromise.'

'Compromise? I have no intention of making

any sort of compromise, and by the way, you have seventy-nine seconds left!'

'Thank you. Look, you can't still believe that ridiculous theory about me! Surely you've realised that you've made a mistake now you've had chance to sleep on it? I mean, do I seem the sort of man who would allow a woman to keep him?'

'Yes, I do . . . no, I've not made any sort of mistake, and yes, as far as I am concerned you fit the bill exactly!'

'So you've no intention of reconsidering and maybe dropping the case?'

'None whatsoever. Forty seconds.'

'What if I threaten to go to Margaret and tell her what's going on?'

'That's your decision entirely,' she said, her heart sinking at the thought of the trouble it would cause with her client. Mr Johnson had been so adamant about the need for discretion, and there was no way he would consider she'd fulfilled that request if he found out exactly what had happened. It could damage her reputation irrevocably. She had to know if Maxwell intended to do it. She swallowed hard, forcing a cool disinterest to her tone. 'Will you?'

'No.'

'Because you're frightened of losing a valuable meal ticket,' she scoffed, and heard him draw a deep, furious breath.

'No, damn you! I won't tell Margaret because I don't want her to get hurt by finding out in such an unsavoury manner that her husband doesn't trust her.'

Just for a moment, his answer threw her. He sounded so sincere, as though he really meant it, but then of course he would, wouldn't he? Sounding sincere was his stock-in-trade.

'A fine sentiment, Mr Maxwell. It would do you credit if I was silly enough to believe it. Now, I think your time is just about up. Thank you for calling, but don't bother to do it again. I shall be out in future.'

'What if I need to engage your services at any time?'

'Then I suggest you call my secretary and let her fix up an appointment. I'm sure I'll be able to fit you in some time in the next ten years.'

He laughed softly, lightly, a ripple of sound which made something in Martha curl up in unexpected pleasure.

'I'm not going to give up, Martha Clark. Somehow I'm going to convince you that you're wrong about me, and do you know what?'

'What?' she asked, suddenly wary.

'It's going to be a pleasure, a real pleasure. I'll be seeing you, Martha. Soon. Take care.'

'Now look here . . .'

He'd cut the connection. For a few seconds Martha sat and stared at the phone till the dull hum of the dialling tone broke the spell. She replaced the receiver, feeling more uneasy than ever. What did he mean, he was going to convince her? She didn't want convincing. She wanted to believe all the bad things she could about Quinn Maxwell because it was the only way she could protect herself from the man.

She was right about him . . . right, right, right! The word echoed round and round in her head time and again, yet instead of gaining strength from the repetition it seemed to take on a hint of desperation. She was right about him; she just had to be!

Lunchtime came and went, but Martha stayed at her desk, ignoring the hungry growlings of her stomach. Most days when she was in the office she walked down to the delicatessen on the corner for a sandwich and coffee, but today she didn't feel like going out. She wanted to keep her mind busy, keep it so occupied with work that she wouldn't have time to dwell on what Maxwell had said over the phone. He was George Bryant's problem now, and she had to remember that, but it was a strangely difficult task. If she just let her mind wander for the tiniest moment, then he had a way of sneaking into her thoughts again. He was driving her mad!

So hour after hour she sat at her desk, keeping her mind centred on her work with a steely determination, till finally she knew she just had to go home. Her head was throbbing from the constant strain, her body aching with tiredness she could ignore no longer. Like it or not, she would have to stop work now, or she would be in danger of cracking up, and there was no way she would give that tiresome man the satisfaction of making her do that!

Jeannie had left some time before, so Martha locked up the office, then made her way slowly through the near-deserted building to the back street where she'd left her car. She unlocked the door and slid inside, resting wearily back against the seat for a few seconds before starting the engine with a sigh. Somehow the prospect of going home to her quiet flat with only her thoughts for company was strangely unappealing, yet the alternatives were even worse. She didn't want to sit in a restaurant or cinema by herself while all around her people were together. It would only make her feel more alone than ever.

She drove slowly across the city, glad that most of the dreadful rush-hour traffic was gone. She didn't feel up to coping with that sort of hassle tonight. When she got home she went straight in and ran the bath, adding a generous measure of bubble-bath to the steaming water. Hopefully a long soak would soothe the headache away and revive her enough to see out the evening. She'd eaten nothing all day, and she knew she should really make herself a meal, or at least a sandwich, but somehow it all seemed like too much of an effort. Maybe she'd feel like it after the bath.

Leaving the taps running, she walked through to the bedroom and stripped off her clothes, pulling a soft fleecy robe over her chilled body. The central heating had been switched off all day and the flat was cold, but it wasn't only that which sent these icy shivers racing down her backbone. It stemmed more from this horrible feeling of aloneness which threatened to overwhelm her. It had been ages since she'd felt like this, and it made her feel so very vulnerable to experience it again.

She crossed to the mirror and brushed her hair back from her face, catching it up at the sides with two tortoiseshell slides, then paused to study her reflection. In the stark glare of the overhead light her face was very pale, dark shadows staining the delicate skin under eyes which were almost feverishly bright. Just a week ago her life had been running smoothly, yet now she felt as though everything she'd striven for was in danger of crumbling around her. If that happened, then she would be left with nothing: nothing but the emptiness which had haunted her for years since Paul had died, and there was no way she could face that again. Somehow she had to get a grip on herself and not allow that to happen.

Turning away from the mirror, she retraced her steps to the bathroom and slipped off the robe, ready to climb into the steaming water. The doorbell rang and she cursed aloud in sudden annoyance. Why did it always have to happen just when she'd run a bath? She could go weeks without a caller, yet as soon as she went to step into the bath, either the doorbell or the telephone would ring. Well, tonight she wasn't going to answer it. Whoever it was could just go away. She was in no mood for visitors tonight.

She stepped into the water, murmuring in pleasure as heat flowed through her cold limbs, making them tingle. She leant back and closed her eyes, then snapped them open again as the bell rang a second time, longer, louder, as though the uninvited caller was becoming impatient. Martha's face tightened with annoyance, her green eyes sparking. Couldn't they take a hint and go away? Determinedly she slithered deeper into the water, feeling the bubbles brushing softly against her chin. Sheer bliss!

The bell rang again, long, strident rings, demanding attention, and with a snarl of anger Martha hauled herself to her feet. She patted herself roughly dry, then dragged on her robe. So help her, whoever was leaning on the bell like that was going to be sorry! She stormed through the flat, tracking wet footprints across the carpet, and wrenched open the front door.

'Yes! What do you want?' Her voice was sharp with anger and the man standing outside took a hasty step backwards, obviously startled.

'Er . . . Ms Clark?' he stammered nervously, consulting a piece of paper in his shaking hand.

'Yes,' she snapped, glaring at him.

'Dinner.'

'Pardon?'

For a long second Martha stared at him, wondering if he'd gone mad or if there was something wrong with her hearing.

'Your order for dinner,' he repeated patiently,

motioning sideways with his hand. Martha's jaw dropped as she suddenly spotted the laden dinner trolley with its gleaming crystal and wafer-thin china. For a moment shock robbed her of the ability to speak, but it was only a momentary affliction.

'I didn't order any dinner. There must be a mistake.'

Her green eyes were cold, her voice icy, and the man flinched, shooting a desperate glance at his paper, then at the flat door.

'This is number eight, and the name is Clark, isn't it?'

'Yes and yes! But I repeat, I didn't order any dinner, so you had better take it away.' She stepped back to slam the door, then stopped as he spoke, words which made her go rigid with a dawning comprehension.

'I'm sorry, madam, but this is definitely the address Mr Maxwell gave us, so I can't see how there's been any mistake. Could it be some sort of a surprise for you?'

'Maxwell,' she repeated slowly, her mind suddenly numb. 'Quinn Maxwell?'

'Oh, so you do know him. Good.' There was an expression of deep relief on the man's face now, a relief which faded the instant Martha spoke again.

'Know him! Too right I know him. The sneaky, low-down, good-for-nothing——'

'Tut, tut, Martha. Is that any way to talk about the man who not only sends you flowers but dinner as well?'

The low, mocking voice cut her off dead. Martha spun round, her eyes widening as she spotted Quinn Maxwell standing in the hallway. She'd been so incensed to learn that he was behind all this that she'd never even noticed him arriving. Now she rounded on him, her green eyes spitting venom.

'Now, you look here, Quinn Maxwell, if you think you can keep this up, harassing me this way, then you can think again! There are laws to stop people like you, d'you hear me?'

'Now that is interesting: laws to prevent harassment. I must get my solicitor to look into that, Martha.'

His voice was cold, crackling like chips of ice, and Martha hesitated. The last thing the agency needed was a law suit and all its attendant publicity. It would scare away any prospective or long-term clients faster than the plague. She snapped her lips shut and glared at him, wondering what was going to happen next. For in this instance there was no doubt that he was calling all the shots.

'Well, I'm glad that you've decided to be sensible.' He nodded to the hovering waiter. 'Please take the trolley in.'

With a marked ill-grace Martha stepped aside while the man wheeled the trolley inside and laid out cutlery and china with a haste which spoke volumes. Within minutes he had finished, and Quinn Maxwell closed the door behind him. He turned to face her, his grey eyes unfathomable as they studied her across the width of the room, and all of a sudden Martha realised just what a sight she must look with her hair snatched back and her face devoid of any make-up. She pulled the robe tighter round her damp body, quite unaware of how the fabric clung to every soft curve and line. Her mind was racing, skittering first this way then that as she tried to work out how to handle the situation, but there didn't seem to be any easy answers.

'You look nervous, Martha.'

His soft mockery was just what she needed to whip her senses into order, and she stood up straighter, her eyes flashing.

'Just tell me what you want and then get out. I've had all I can take of you today, one way and another.'

'Have you, indeed?'

His voice was a low purr of soft sound and Martha moved nervously, something about the tone of his deep voice making her wary. She stared back at him, flushing as she met his steady gaze. There was something in the depths of his eyes, a flicker of awareness, which made her want to run from the room and hide. He might only be doing this to scare her off, make her change her mind about handling the case, but the way he was watching her told a different story. He wasn't seeing her as the enemy at this moment, but as a woman, and the realisation terrified her.

There was silence in the room, a deep, tense

silence which Martha couldn't seem to find the strength to break, no matter how much she wanted to. They just stood there, linked by a strange invisible bond of tension, an awareness of each other as man and woman. Then he spoke, mundane words which broke the spell.

'Why don't you sit down and eat before the food gets cold?'

The pent-up breath eased from her body in a jerky little flow, and she thrust her chin out at an unconsciously belligerent angle.

'I'm not hungry, and even if I were, I wouldn't touch a mouthful of that meal.'

'Pity.' He crossed the room to lift the silver-domed lid off the serving platter. 'Marcel's is one of the best restaurants in town, and it smells delicious.'

A fragrant waft came from the trolley, and Martha felt her stomach knot up ready to rumble in appreciative hunger, but there was no way even a morsel of the food would pass her lips.

'If it's so good, then take it home with you. I don't want it. I'm sure I can find you a bag to put it all in. Now, I repeat, what do you want? I was taking a bath.'

'So I can see,' he murmured, his eyes tracing over her slender figure in the clinging robe with a devilish sparkle in their silver depths. Instantly Martha wished she'd never drawn attention to herself that way. Warmth stole under the fine pale skin of her throat and she looked away, unable to handle this sort of baiting. Sexual banter was something she knew little about and couldn't handle. It made her go hot all over to realise he knew she was wearing nothing under the robe, as though she was allowing him liberties she'd allowed no man apart from Paul.

She thrust her hands deep into the pockets of the robe to hide their trembling. She wouldn't allow him to see just how much he affected her. It made her far too vulnerable.

'I have no intention of standing here playing games with you like this. If you can't tell me why you've come, then I suggest that you leave.'

She started towards the door, halting as he made no attempt to move out of her way. He just stood his ground, his eyes tracing slowly over her, a strangely gentle expression on his face.

'Why are you afraid of me, Martha?' he asked softly.

'Afraid? Of course I'm not afraid of you. Don't flatter yourself.' Her voice was strangely high-pitched and breathless, quite unlike her usually controlled tones, and she bit her lip in vexation. He laughed, a low, deep laugh which sent a tingling curl of sensation up her backbone.

'Oh, come on, Martha, why lie? I can see it in your face. You're afraid of me, but why? You know quite well that I won't hurt you physically.'

He stepped forwards, narrowing the gap between them, and Martha felt her pulse race at the gentleness in his voice. She looked down, staring at her bare toes peeping from under the hem of the long robe, wishing she were dressed.

Maybe she would have been able to handle the situation better hidden behind the barrier of clothes, but then again, just who was she kidding? She would need armour against this man, nothing less.

'Why, Martha?' It was obvious that he had no intention of letting the matter drop, so she would have to answer.

'Of course I'm wary of you,' she said haltingly. 'Who wouldn't be, after all that's happened? I just can't understand what you hope to achieve by all this. Do you really think that you can make me change my mind by bribing me with flowers and dinner?' She deliberately whipped up her anger, taking refuge behind it from a situation which was far more dangerous than any she'd encountered.

'Perhaps. I don't know. Maybe I just wanted to show you that I'm not the sort of man that you think I am.'

'Well, this won't achieve anything. The best way of convincing me is by stopping seeing Mrs Johnson and the others. Then I can call a halt to this whole thing.'

'And what happens to all the reports you've already made? All those dates and details, notes of people coming and going at my house. Will you destroy them, even give them to me, or will you pass them on to whoever's paying your fee?'

'I . . .' For some reason she couldn't understand, she couldn't lie to him, even to save a scene. 'I shall have to pass them on, of course.

The information isn't mine, it belongs to my client.'

'And what if he then decides that his wife *is* having an affair with me? What will you do then? Sit back and let it destroy their marriage?' There was an icy, biting contempt in his voice which was so unjust that it made her furious.

'*I* am not ruining their marriage, you are!'

'So you say, but what's the evidence? A few visits to my house, the suspicions of a man who is obviously more prepared to believe the worst of his wife than trust her?'

'Surely it's only natural for Mr Johnson to be suspicious? If his wife has nothing to hide, then why doesn't she tell him about her visits and explain the reason for them?'

'Why should she? Surely she's entitled to some privacy, entitled to his trust without having to give written guarantees. That's what marriage is all about, after all, love and trust, but then I doubt if you've had much chance to find that out in your profession.'

'You're a fine one to talk about love and trust, Quinn Maxwell!' she snapped, stung into replying. 'How many marriages have you broken up, and all with those same high ideals?'

'None, but I don't expect you to believe that.' He ran his hands through his hair, as though suddenly weary of the whole conversation. 'Look, Martha, I didn't come here tonight to argue, I came to see if we could reach some sort of an understanding over a leisurely dinner.'

'Never. We're not on the same wavelength. There's no understanding we can ever reach.'

'So it seems, but how about dinner? Can't we at least sit down and get to know each other a little better?'

'No.'

'Oh, Martha, surely you wouldn't deny a hungry man some food, would you? I took the liberty of ordering for two.' He nodded towards the trolley, and Martha shot it a quick glance, her temper flaring as she realised he'd done just that. The nerve of the man, to think that she would share a meal with him after all that had gone on!

'Yes, I could deny you food. I could deny you water in a desert, and with the greatest pleasure. Now, goodnight. Thank you for the dinner. I shall eat it after all and enjoy every mouthful. I seem to have regained my appetite.'

He chuckled softly. 'So hard, so tough, little Martha, but are you really?'

'That is something you will never know. Goodnight!'

She swung the door open, waiting with a mounting impatience for him to leave, her pulse leaping as he stopped just inches from her. In the soft light his eyes were silvery as he stared down at her, reflecting tiny images of herself in their gleaming depths.

'Goodnight, Martha. In a way, I'm glad you've decided to make a fight of it. It means that I have a real excuse for seeing you again.' Slowly he bent his head, brushing her lips with his, so fleetingly that she had no chance to turn away. Then he was gone, walking down the hall without a backward glance.

Martha closed the door, clinging hold of the lock as her legs threatened to buckle. She raised her hand, touching her fingers to her lips, feeling the lingering echo of warmth from that brief, surprisingly sweet kiss. Tears filled her eyes and ran slowly down her cheeks, but she wasn't even aware of them.

It had been so long since a man had kissed her that way . . . so very long.

CHAPTER SIX

ANOTHER restless night had taken its toll, adding to the pallor of her skin and deepening the shadows under her eyes. Ruthlessly Martha went to work on her face, determined to obliterate the signs of Quinn Maxwell's handiwork. She'd spent most of the previous day thinking about him and yet another night dreaming about him. Where would it all end?

She briskly applied a second coat of rose blusher to her cheeks, fluffing it up over the curve of her temples to give a much-needed glow to her pale face. She had several appointments booked for that morning, and a pale, wan face would never inspire confidence in prospective clients.

She was at her desk working when Jeannie arrived, and was instantly glad that she'd taken so much trouble with her appearance when she saw the look her secretary shot her way. Two late arrivals at the office had obviously fired the girl's imagination, and Martha didn't need to be much of a detective to know which way it was running. If only Jeannie knew the truth! Oh, granted, it was a man who had been the cause of her recent tardiness, but not in the way the irrepressibly romantic Jeannie thought. There was no way her relationship with Quinn Maxwell could be classed as romantic by any stretch of even the most vivid imagination!

The morning wore slowly on, and in between seeing clients Martha kept returning to the new case, trying to pinpoint the elusive little clue which still evaded her. It was there, somewhere in the furthest corner of her mind, if she could only draw it out. Time and again she read over the report, till she could repeat each page word-perfect, but still it refused to surface. Maybe a visit to the gallery where the robbery had taken place would give it the jolt it needed.

She slid on her coat and left the office, pausing briefly to tell Jeannie where she was going. Outside the air was cold and deliciously crisp, the nip of frost welcome after the stuffy heat inside, and impulsively Martha decided to leave her car behind and walk. It was just over a mile into the centre of town, far enough to blow the cobwebs away, yet not so far as to make it a chore.

She took her time, walking slowly as she peered into the shop windows along the way, studying their seasonal red and gold displays, and gradually she became aware of that tiny ache of loneliness growing inside her once again. In a few weeks' time it would be Christmas, a time of merriment and happiness for most people, yet she knew it wouldn't be like that for her. All Christmas meant to her was a few empty days alone in the flat without even the distraction of work to make the hours pass. Somehow the prospect seemed even less appealing than usual.

She quickened her pace, deliberately trying to wipe the depressing thought from her mind, and in a very short time arrived at the exclusive gallery in the centre of town. She walked inside, smiling at the receptionist seated at the discreetly expensive desk in the foyer.

'May I help you, madam?' the girl enquired courteously, but Martha shook her head.

'I just wanted to look around, see if anything catches my eye,' she answered evasively. No one at the gallery was aware that the claim had been passed to her for investigation, and there was no way she wanted them to know. All too often it was the element of surprise which was the deciding factor in a case.

The girl smiled and handed her a catalogue before turning her attention back to the papers on the desk, and Martha walked quickly through the reception area into the first room. She already knew from the scale plans she'd been given that there were three rooms to the gallery, and that it was from the third room, the one furthest away from the main door, that the paintings had disappeared. What she wanted to check on now was how long it took to walk the distance from the rear of the premises to the front. Surely it couldn't be the twenty minutes that the guard had claimed, even allowing for the fact he might have stopped en route. That was the part of the report which bothered her most.

Not wanting to draw attention to herself, Martha walked slowly round the first room, stopping briefly at several of the paintings while she made a show of consulting the catalogue. There were a few other people in the gallery, talking in low, hushed voices, but she carefully kept well clear of them, not wanting to get involved in conversation.

'Darling, it's perfect. It would look marvellous over your bed. You must let me buy it for you.'

The woman's voice, though not loud, cut through the muted murmurs and instinctively Martha glanced round, her eyes widening as she caught sight of the couple in the far corner. For a moment she stood rooted to the spot, too surprised to consider the wisdom of her action.

The woman had her back towards her, but even from this angle Martha could see that she was beautifully and expensively dressed, her figure trim, her silver hair immaculately groomed. Yet it wasn't she who held Martha's attention but the man standing beside her, his dark gold hair gleaming in the glow from an angled spotlight: Quinn Maxwell.

As though sensing her gaze, he looked round and Martha felt her pulse leap as she met his eyes across the width of the room. For a long, timeless moment they stared at each other, a strange tension claiming them both, then the woman spoke again and Martha felt herself go cold with an icy contempt as she heard her.

'Quinn, you're not paying attention to me. I

said I'll buy the painting for you, if you'd like it. A little Christmas present from me.' She let her hand drop to his arm in a caressing little gesture, and Martha felt her stomach churn with a sudden lurching sickness. She'd known all along what he did and how he made a living, yet somehow it was devastating to see the actual evidence of it.

She turned away, hurrying from the room, not hearing the receptionist's solicitous enquiry if there was anything the matter. All she knew was that she had to get out, get away from the sight of Quinn Maxwell and that woman together before she was sick.

She ran out to the street and stood staring blankly up and down, her mind too numb with the shock of what she'd witnessed to function properly. She felt cold, icy, as though a thousand slivers of ice were trickling through her bloodstream, chilling her to the bone. How could he do it? How could he degrade himself in such a manner? Last night, after he'd kissed her, that sweet, tender little kiss, she'd almost wanted to believe that she'd been as wrong about him as he'd said, but now she knew she'd been stupid. Quinn Maxwell was everything she'd thought him to be and probably more, and the realisation hurt her in a way she'd never expected. Somehow she felt as though he'd betrayed her.

'Martha! Wait a minute. Don't go!'

The sound of his voice cut through the numbness. Martha shot a swift look over her shoulder at the man hurrying towards her, then took to her heels, uncaring what he thought of her actions. She didn't want to talk to him, not now, not ever. Not after what she'd just seen. She'd made no mistake about him; he was a gigolo and she wanted nothing more to do with him.

Ruthlessly she elbowed her way through the crowds of shoppers, ignoring the startled glances, the barely heard mutters of protest as she pushed them aside. She could hear footsteps behind her, pounding on the pavement, and she ran faster, determined to evade him. A few yards ahead a taxi pulled in to the kerb for a passenger to alight, and Martha hurried towards it, realising it was her only chance of getting away. She would never be able to outrun him, even with the few yards' start she had.

'Damn it, Martha, stop! This is crazy.' The breathlessly roared order was just what she needed to make that final effort. She lengthened her stride, putting everything she had into the last few yards' sprint towards the cab, then cried out in alarm as her heel caught in a narrow crack in the paving slabs. She fell forwards, bruising her palms and her knees as she hit the floor with a jolting force, and lay quite still, stunned by the impact.

'Are you all right?' In a trice he was down on his knees beside her, his hands gentle as he lifted her into a sitting position. 'Oh, hell! Just look what you've done, you crazy woman.'

He pulled a clean handkerchief out of his

pocket and gently mopped at the bloody cuts on her hands, the raw, angry grazes on both her knees, while Martha sat dazedly watching him.

'For heaven's sake, Martha, why did you do such a stupid thing? You could have really hurt yourself, running off like that.' There was anger in his voice and Martha blinked, trying to regather her scattered senses. The unexpected speed and force of the fall had shaken her, but she couldn't just sit here on the pavement and let him minister to her. She pushed his hands away and struggled to her feet, wincing as pain sliced through her bruised, tender flesh. A small crowd had gathered to watch the proceedings, and Martha summoned up a rather shaky smile for their benefit.

'I'm all right, thank you,' she said, to no one in particular, then picked up her bag from the pavement, aware that Maxwell was watching her closely. She should really say something to him, something to explain and dismiss her actions, yet the words seemed to be lodged in her throat. She just looked up at him, seeing his face harden at the contempt he could read in her eyes.

'You've got it wrong, Martha,' he said softly. 'Once again you've misinterpreted the facts.'

'I don't know what you mean,' she said shortly, turning to head back up the street.

'Don't give me that, sweetheart. I'm not blind or stupid. I know full well what you're thinking; I knew it back in the gallery.'

'Do you? Good, because now there's no need to

say anything more, is there?' She stopped and glared up at him, her eyes hard and overly bright, like pieces of green glass. 'Don't you think you'd better get back to your "friend"? I'm sure she won't take kindly to being left like that. It might make her decide not to buy you that expensive picture, and then you'd lose a valuable investment.'

For a moment anger darkened his eyes, turning them to a deep stormy grey, then he seemed to make a deliberate effort to wipe it away. He smiled at her, a taunting, teasing little smile, which whipped a fresh surge of colour to her cheeks. 'Does the idea of my having "friends", as you delicately put it, bother you that much?'

Martha turned her face away, desperate to hide her expression from his too discerning gaze. It bothered her, all right, though why, she couldn't for the life of her imagine, but there was no way she was going to admit it to him. She swallowed hard, forcing back her own anger and that strange feeling of betrayal.

'I don't care how many women you have, quite frankly. You can have a different one for every day of the week, plus two for Sundays, as far as I'm concerned. So don't kid yourself that it bothers me one bit!'

She walked away, forcing herself not to stumble as her stiffening knees protested at the sudden turn of speed.

'Wait a minute. My car's only down the road. I'll drive you back wherever you want to go.

You're in no fit state to walk.' He caught her arm in an attempt to steer her down a side street, but Martha wrenched herself free, her body stiff with anger.

'I don't need your help, thank you. I can manage by myself.'

'I'm sure you can, but why bother when I'm willing to help you? If I didn't know better I'd say that you were still upset about what you saw, and that's the reason you won't be sensible.'

'Of course I'm not upset. Don't be ridiculous!' she snapped. 'I've already told you that I don't care what you do or with whom you do it.'

'Well, then, prove it and let me drive you back. Why make such a fuss about it?' He glanced up at the sky which had suddenly changed from its former sparkling blue to a heavy leaden grey. 'Come on, let's not waste any more time arguing over something so trivial. It looks as if it's going to rain any minute.'

There was an expression on his face which brooked no more arguments, and Martha knew the easiest thing now would be to agree. After all, it was only a mile or so to her office, no distance at all by car, so what was the point in making a fuss about it? In silence she followed him along the street and let him help her into the car, biting back a groan of relief as she straightened her aching knees. She eased the hem of her coat up an inch or two and stared at the grazed, purpling flesh wryly. It had been years since she'd taken such a tumble—when she was a child and scarred knees had been an everyday hazard. The trouble was, she was now twenty years older and twenty years stiffer! She'd be lucky if she could walk in the morning.

'You'll need to bathe those cuts thoroughly when you get back. There's still some dirt in them.'

Martha hastily dropped her hemline, flushing slightly as she realised he was paying as much attention to her legs as she was. He chuckled softly, spotting her embarrassed confusion, but said nothing more as he started the engine and eased the car out into the traffic.

'Where to?' he asked briefly.

'My office. It's in Jersey Street, just off——'

'I know where it is,' he said shortly, and Martha sat back in the seat, refusing to ask him how he knew. She had an idea she wouldn't like the answer. Quinn Maxwell seemed to know far more about her than she cared for.

The sleek car ate up the distance, so that it was bare minutes before they pulled up outside the imposing building which housed her office. He cut the engine, then turned to face her, his eyes unreadable as they traced over her face. Suddenly self-conscious, Martha smoothed her hair back from her face, unwittingly smearing a trail of dirt up the side of her cheek from her grubby hand. Why was he watching her like that, staring at her as though he was storing up impressions of her? It made her feel intensely aware of him.

'I——' she began, but stopped as he spoke

almost at the same moment.

'So, how do you feel now?' he asked with a genuine concern. 'Are your hands very sore?'

She glanced down at her cut and grubby palms, staring at the angry red marks for a few seconds while she tried to grab hold of her composure. There had been so much tenderness in his voice just then, such caring, that it had thrown her completely.

'They're all right,' she finally managed to answer huskily. 'Still sore, of course, but they'll be fine in a couple of days.'

'They're bound to be sore after the tumble you took. What on earth made you run off like that, Martha?'

What could she say? For a few helpless minutes Martha floundered round, trying to find some sort of acceptable answer, anything at all other than the truth.

'I . . . well, I was in the gallery on business. When I saw you I was worried that you would say something that could reveal who I was. It seemed safer to make a hasty exit.' It sounded plausible, but would he believe her? Holding her breath, she waited to find out.

'I see. So you were working on a case, were you? And your sudden flight had nothing to do with seeing my "friend" and me together, then?' he asked, with a light mockery which made Martha wriggle uncomfortably in her seat.

'No. Of course not! I've already told you that what you do is entirely your own concern. Now, I think I'd better be getting inside. Thank you for driving me back. It was kind of you, in the circumstances.' She unclipped her seat-belt, desperate to get away before he asked any more awkward questions, and gasped in alarm as he caught her chin in a gentle clasp, turning her to face him.

'What do you think you're——'

'Shhh, stay still a minute. You've got a smudge on your cheek. I'll wipe it off for you.'

With the utmost delicacy he rubbed the pad of his thumb over the soft curve of her cheek, stroking her skin in a light caress which sent flurries of sensation tingling through her body.

'There, that's better. It wouldn't do for the staff to see you looking as though you'd been in a fight, now, would it?' He ran his fingers down her cheek in a final gentle motion and Martha hastily pulled back, terrified of what he might read in her expression. She caught hold of her bag, staring down at it as though she found the cut and shape of the grey leather fascinating. It was difficult to think straight while every cell in her body was still tingling, but she had to try. She couldn't let him see how much his touch had shaken her.

'Thank you, and thank you again for driving me back, Mr Maxwell.' There was only the faintest tremble to her voice, and she felt quite pleased with herself for the effort.

'Don't mention it. It was the least I could do.' He glanced out of the window, his eyes narrowing as he stared thoughtfully up at the tall office block. 'Nice place. A good spot for an office, I imagine. Close to town, yet not too close to have to put up with all the noise and hustle.'

'It suits my needs. Well, I won't detain you any longer. I'm sure your friend must be wondering where you've got to.' She slid out of the car as quickly as her stiff legs would let her, then bent rather awkwardly to close the door. Reaching out, he stopped it from closing, his eyes silvery as he smiled up at her.

'Don't worry about that, Martha. I'm sure she'll be quite happy to wait for me. Now, don't forget what I said: make sure you bathe those cuts well. I'd hate to think of anything marring those beautiful legs.'

Before she could think up a reply to this bit of sheer impertinence, he slammed the car door and pulled away from the kerb. Martha stared after him, oblivious to the big cold drops of rain which had started to fall. He was impossible, totally and utterly impossible, yet she knew with a sinking feeling that there would be more than one woman prepared to wait for him, no matter how long he took!

CHAPTER SEVEN

THAT George Bryant was good at his job was a fact Martha had long been aware of. Now, however, staring down at the neatly typed papers on her desk, she could see the tangible evidence of his expertise. He had missed nothing out of his reports on Quinn Maxwell's exploits, and Martha felt herself go hot all over as she read her name on several of the pages.

What on earth must George think about it all? First there had been that strange night-time visit to her flat, then yesterday's drive back to the office, all neatly logged and carefully presented in indisputable black and white. Thank heavens that the ever-correct George obviously saw it as none of his business. If he'd questioned her, Martha knew she would be hard pushed to find an explanation for her unethical behaviour.

With a sigh she slid the reports back into their folder and filed them away, determined not to waste any more time on the case. One way and another, Quinn Maxwell had already claimed more than his share of her attention, and although she should really start writing her interim report on the case, Martha knew she wasn't going to do it today. Today she had the sneakiest feeling that any comments or opinions she might make would be extremely biased, and that would never do. She owed it to herself and her clients to make her observations in a suitably objective and professional manner. Cutting remarks were most definitely out!

The day was busy, though Martha spent most of it out of the office after the first hour. A couple of appointments and a business lunch ran on far longer than she'd expected, yet by the time she checked back into the office in the late afternoon she was feeling much more like her usual competent self. One of the larger insurance groups had asked her to cover a huge claim which needed investigating, and she had been paid very handsomely from the diamond job. Allied to that, the grateful owner of the jewels had extended an invitation to a party he was holding later in the month, and rather to her surprise Martha had accepted. It had been ages since she'd been to anything as exciting as this ritzy party, and she was looking forward to it immensely. It was about time she started to get out and about a bit.

With the cheque safely stowed in her bag and her mind full of the new dress she would buy for the occasion, she breezed into the office.

Jeannie was at her desk typing when she walked in, and she grinned at Martha, her pleasant face filled with excitement.

'Well, you look pleased with yourself,' Martha said, smiling. 'What's happened?' She picked up a pile of message slips and flicked through them, discarding most of them into the bin.

'You'll never guess, Ms Clark, but someone's moved in to the offices next door.'

'Oh, what a shame.'

'Shame? What do you mean?' Jeannie asked, puzzled.

'I had been hoping to take those offices myself. We could do with more space now that the business is expanding. But I suppose it can't be helped. Who's moved in, and why has it sent you into such a flutter?' She sat down on the edge of the desk, kicking off her high-heeled shoes while she wriggled her cramped toes, wincing slightly as the bruises on her poor knees started to twinge.

'Oh, just wait till you see him, then you'll understand.' There was a dreamy look to Jeannie's brown eyes now.

'I see. It's not so much the fact that someone has moved in, but who that someone is. What's he like: tall, dark and handsome?' There was a teasing lightness to Martha's voice, and Jeannie blushed, but it was obvious she wasn't going to be deterred from her news.

'No, or at least, he's not dark. He's gorgeous. Tall, about six feet one, very blond, and with the most beautiful grey eyes you've ever seen. Wow! Just wait till you meet him, Ms Clark. He's everything you could ever dream of in a ma . . . Ms Clark!'

Jeannie's gasp of surprise followed Martha out of the door and along the corridor. She stopped at the adjoining suite, her heart pounding sickeningly as she thrust the door open. It couldn't be him, please heaven, it just couldn't be!

The room was empty apart from yards and yards of new pale green carpet, but Martha didn't stop long enough to admire it. At a run she crossed the room and flung the door to the inner office open so hard that it bounced back on its hinges.

'Why, Martha, what a lovely surprise! How nice of you to drop in to welcome me like this.'

Her heart was pounding so hard that she couldn't seem to catch her breath. She just stood in the doorway and stared at the man comfortably seated behind a huge mahogany desk, his grey eyes watching her with a mocking glitter in their depths. He stood up, moving to a side table which held a selection of decanters and a silver wine cooler.

'Champagne?' he asked, holding the frosted bottle aloft. 'Just to celebrate the fact that we are now neighbours.'

She swallowed hard, her fingers gripping the doorframe as she tried to catch hold of her reeling senses. This couldn't be happening. It must be a dream, a dreadful nightmare. Any minute now she would wake up and find the room empty, and Quinn Maxwell gone.

'Here, drink this. You look as though you could use it.' He held a tulip-shaped glass towards her and Martha stared at it, watching the bubbles in the pale wine rise and cluster on the surface. She could hear the faint hiss they were making, could smell the delicate bouquet of the wine, and knew it was no dream. It was real. He was really here!

She swung round on her stockinged heels and strode from the room, hearing him laugh softly as he watched her go. She was shaking, trembling with anger and a fine tight thread of tension which made her feel light-headed and sick. She walked back to her office and sat down at the desk, resting her head in her hands. How could she cope with this new development? How could she work, knowing he was next door?

There was a soft tapping on the door and hastily Martha composed her features, terrified of letting anyone see what she was feeling.

'Come in.'

'I thought you might like some coffee, Ms Clark.'

Jeannie carefully set a cup of coffee on her desk and Martha smiled faintly at her before picking it up and cradling it in her shaking hands. She'd done a course in first aid once, and she could still remember the instructor's voice barking out the symptoms of shock: pale, cold, clammy, rapid pulse . . . well, that described to the letter how she was feeling. She was in shock, deep shock, and she didn't know how to pull herself out of it.

'Is there anything I can do for you, Ms Clark? Shall I call a doctor?'

Jeannie was watching her with concern on her face, and Martha forced herself to summon up another smile. She shook her head, then sipped the coffee, feeling it inch its way down her tight throat. She had to think, had to make herself find a solution to this problem, if there was one.

She drank again, feeling the warmth start to spread through her body and ease the numbing cold from her limbs. Quinn Maxwell couldn't just come in here and rent office space like this to annoy her. He had to have some sort of legitimate business reason, otherwise it was against the terms of his contract. Was that the loophole she could use to have him evicted? It was a ray of hope, a faint one, admittedly, but better than total darkness.

'There is something you can do for me, Jeannie. Can you get me Drinkwater's on the phone, please?'

'The leasing agents?'

'Yes, please. The number is in the file. I want to speak to Mr Drinkwater himself, though—no one else.'

'Right away.'

Jeannie went away to place the call and Martha drank the rest of her coffee, waiting impatiently for the phone to ring.

'Mr Drinkwater on the line for you, Ms Clark.'

'Thank you. Good afternoon, Mr Drinkwater, Martha Clark speaking from M.C. Investigations.'

'Hello, Ms Clark. What can I do for you? Have you a problem?'

'Actually, yes. I've just been informed that the

suite of offices adjoining mine has been leased.'

'Yes?' There was a wary note to the man's voice, and Martha chose her words carefully.

'I was just a bit disappointed that you hadn't mentioned it to me. I had been hoping to make an offer for those rooms myself.'

'I see. Well, I'm sorry I didn't know that sooner, Ms Clark. The new client came and asked about them quite out of the blue, and everything has gone through surprisingly quickly. It's just a pity that I wasn't made aware of your interest before.'

'Yes, isn't it? What sort of business is the new tenant going to be running? As you can appreciate, I wouldn't want it to be anything which might have a detrimental effect on my own business.'

'You need have no worries on that score, Ms Clark. Mr Maxwell has provided us with the very highest references. He intends to open an investment consultancy there. A thoroughly sound proposition, we feel.'

The man's voice was almost curt, and Martha realised she was getting nowhere. Obviously, Drinkwater's was quite happy to rent the offices rather than have them standing empty. She thanked him and hung up, leaning back in her seat as she tried to come up with some other idea to make Quinn Maxwell decide to leave, but short of fire, flood or hurricane there was nothing she could think of. He was here now, and, if she knew anything at all about him, here to stay, at least until she agreed to fall in with his demands for a compromise. In that case, then, it looked like they were going to be neighbours for some time to come, because there was no way on this earth that she was going to do that!

He was everywhere. In the lift of a morning, in the corridor, crossing the street when she arrived or left the office; everywhere Martha turned, Quinn Maxwell seemed to be there. She tried to ignore him, cutting him dead and staring through him, but the strain on her nerves was starting to tell.

He'd been in residence just four days now, four days which felt like four long years to Martha. Even now, sitting at her desk, working, she was aware of him in the next room. She could hear the murmur of his voice, not actual words, just the ebb and flow of his deep tones, and it disturbed her.

She switched on the small radio on her desk to drown the sound, tuning in to a pop music show and turning the volume up to an ear-splitting level, but it was hardly the thing to aid concentration. With a mutter of annoyance she switched it off and picked up her bag, looping the strap over her shoulder as she walked from the room.

'I'm going to lunch now, Jeannie. I won't be long.'

'Yes, Ms Clark.' Jeannie barely glanced up from the typewriter, her face set, and Martha bit back a sigh. She had been getting the cold shoulder the whole morning, and she couldn't really blame the girl. She'd been less than the perfect boss these past few days, snapping at everyone, and Jeannie had borne the brunt of her ill temper. She would have to make it up with her when this whole problem was resolved.

Shrugging the heavy tweed coat round her shoulders, she hurried along the corridor, automatically slowing as she came level with the door to the adjoining offices. Along with a tall, elegantly dressed blonde secretary, Maxwell had acquired a gleaming brass name-plate on his door. Now she stared at it, a cynical light in her eyes. Maxwell Investments . . . well, that was one way to describe how he made a living, she supposed, claiming that 'clients' invested in him, though she doubted if it would pass the Trades Descriptions Act!

The delicatessen was crowded this lunchtime, and Martha had to wait nearly twenty minutes for one of the small tables tucked at the back of the shop. She sat down and gave her order, then glanced round, nodding to several people she knew. A lot of the staff from the nearby offices lunched there, and usually she would join one or other of the groups to chat. However, today she knew she would be poor company.

The waitress set her order down and Martha smiled her thanks before pulling a thin paperback novel out of her bag and settling down to read. A shadow fell over the pages and she glanced up in annoyance, praying it was no one she knew about to join her.

'Mind if I sit here? There doesn't seem to be anywhere else free today.'

Quinn Maxwell eased his long legs under the table and settled himself comfortably without waiting for her to answer.

'Yes, I do mind,' she snapped. 'Go find your own table, you're not sharing mine!'

Her voice had risen several decibels and a couple on the next table turned and looked at them speculatively. Martha felt the colour flood to her cheeks. She leant towards him, her green eyes hot with temper.

'Listen, Maxwell, I'm sick and tired of you hanging around, so get lost.'

'I only asked to share your table, Martha,' he said with an easy laugh. 'Not your bed.'

The girl on the next table giggled, then clamped her hand over her mouth as Martha shot her a quelling look. She looked round, desperately hoping there would be another seat vacant but, of course, every single one was taken. Mouthing a string of silent, colourful curses, she propped the book against the salt cellar and bent her dark head, determined to ignore him.

'Good book?' he asked after some time, biting into a thick beef sandwich with obvious relish. 'Funny, I wouldn't have thought you would go in for that sort of thing.'

'You know nothing about me, or what I like,' she snapped, turning the page, though she couldn't remember one word she'd read of it.

'Oh, I wouldn't say that, Martha. You'd be surprised what I know about you.'

'What do you mean?' Startled, she looked up at him, her eyes mirroring her confusion.

'Well, now, where shall I start? I know where you live, where you work, what sort of music you like, though I was rather surprised at your taste when I heard what you were playing this morning, and now I know what sort of books you like. I'd hardly call that nothing.'

'Well, I would. Now, will you either be quiet or go away? Preferably the latter.' She flicked another page over, staring blindly down at the black print. The table was only small and they were close together, so close that she could feel his knee brush against hers. She moved slightly, easing her legs back from the unwelcome pressure, then wished she hadn't as she saw the knowing expression on his face. It was hopeless. There was no way she could sit here and eat with him just inches away, laughing at her.

She snapped the book closed and thrust it back into her bag before standing up, stumbling slightly as he caught hold of her wrist.

'Where are you going?' he asked quietly. 'You haven't eaten your lunch yet.'

'Anywhere . . . anywhere at all that I can get away from you.' To her surprise and dismay she heard her voice break. She twisted her arm, trying to free it from his hold, but though he only held her gently, his fingers light against her skin, she couldn't seem to break free.

'Sit down, Martha. Finish your lunch and let's call a truce for now. I didn't mean to upset you.'

There was a genuine concern in his eyes as he looked up at her, and Martha sat down abruptly, unable to continue the struggle. She picked up the sandwich and nibbled the edge of it, feeling her throat close as she tried to swallow.

'Relax,' he said softly. 'It's truce time, remember? Time out of the battle.' His voice was gently teasing and she couldn't help but smile. 'That's better. Now, come along, let's find a safe topic to talk about. How about the weather? That's always something the British love to talk about, probably because it's so damned awful.'

His voice was wry and Martha chuckled despite herself. 'True enough, but what do you mean, "the British"? Aren't you one yourself?'

'I suppose I am and I'm not,' he answered, slowly stirring his coffee. 'I was born in Britain, and my parents are British, so technically I am, but I've lived abroad, mainly in Australia, for so long now that it's hard to say if I really feel "British", whatever that is.'

'Australia?' She stared at him, startled. 'I suppose that's where you got that fabulous tan.'

He grinned. 'Too true,' he said in mocking imitation of a thick Aussie accent. 'Boy, do I miss those golden beaches and all that sunshine in this weather.'

'So why are you here?' she asked, her green eyes curious.

He shrugged, his heavy shoulders moving lightly under the grey suit jacket. 'I just felt like a change, wanted to see if I could carve a new life out for myself over here. I had a bad accident in Australia a couple of months back, water-skiing, and was laid up for quite a while. It gave me time to think, to start evaluating what I'd done with my life—and frankly it didn't seem to add up to much.'

There was a pensive look on his face and Martha was intrigued.

'Why? I mean, you seem to be successful. You definitely don't give the appearance of being on your uppers.'

'Oh, I had money; that wasn't the problem, far from it. But it was family money, from what my father had made. I wanted to see if I could strike out for myself.'

'And how are you doing? Or is that the sort of question which will make you lower the white flag?'

He laughed, open amusement on his face, and Martha noticed how several women in the room turned to look at him. It was no wonder; he was handsome enough to make any woman want to turn and look.

'No, we're still in truce time. I'm doing quite well, very well, in fact.'

'And will you stay here, or will you go back some day?'

'That depends,' he answered softly, staring straight into her eyes. Martha swallowed hard, finding it strangely difficult to look away.

'On what?' she whispered.

'On how things work out over the next few weeks.' He reached out and caught her hand, turning it over so that he could trace her palm with a gentle finger. 'Do you believe in fate, Martha? That everything we do is pre-ordained, mapped out as some believe on the palms of our hands?'

She shook her head, feeling the gentle touch of his long finger tingling through her flesh like fire. 'No. Do you?'

'Yes. I think it was fate that made us meet, and it will be fate which binds us together in the future.'

He sounded so sure, so certain, and for one brief, glorious moment Martha pushed all common sense aside, wanting to believe him. Yet how could she? How could she believe a word he said, when all the facts spoke differently? She eased her hand free and stood up, suddenly desperate to leave before she did anything she could only regret in the future.

'Truce over, Martha?' he asked, looking up at her.

'Yes,' she answered. 'Yes, truce over.' And wondered why she suddenly felt so achingly hollow deep inside.

The dress was perfect. Martha knew the moment she laid eyes on it that it was just what she wanted for the party. It was a pale, soft green, the bodice softly draped, the skirt clinging to her slender legs before flaring gently just below the knee. As soon as Martha tried it on in the exclusive boutique, she knew she had to have it, no matter what it cost. It had been ages since she'd bought anything like this filmy drift of fabric. In the past few years her clothes had been chosen for sheer practicality and nothing else, but this dress was different: a beguiling piece of witchery.

She took her time getting ready for the party, first taking a leisurely bath, then concentrating on doing her hair and make-up, but the result was worth it. When she stepped in front of the mirror it was as though she had suddenly stepped back in time.

Since Paul had died she'd spent the barest amount of time possible on her appearance, content to make herself look neat and tidy. Now, studying the reflection in the long mirror, Martha saw again a glimpse of the girl she had once been: small and slender, with fine, pale skin and huge, glowing green eyes, soft as pools of tranquil water. The only difference now was the awareness in her face, an echo of the pain and sorrow she'd had in her life. It hadn't been there three years ago, and now no amount of cosmetics could hide it.

She slipped into her best black coat and fastened the collar tightly round her throat before hurrying out to her car. The night was bitterly cold, a thin, icy wind wailing mournfully through the bare trees, settling a fine skin of ice along the roads. It had been sleeting earlier in the day, and Martha knew she would have to drive carefully. It would be only too easy to hit a patch of ice and skid tonight.

It was a good half-hour drive across the city to the sumptuous house where the party was being held, and Martha breathed a sigh of relief when she finally turned into the drive. There were several dozen cars parked already, mainly huge, expensive limousines, and she gave a wry little laugh as she inched her small economy model into a narrow gap next to a maroon Rolls-Royce. From the look of the vehicles, the evening promised to be everything she'd expected; she only hoped both she and the dress were equal to the occasion!

The front door opened smoothly a bare second after she rang the bell, and she was ushered into an elegant hall by a tail-coated butler. She stared round, her eyes wide as saucers as she took stock of the magnificent chandeliers, the antique furniture, the exquisite paintings. Her host was a Greek shipping owner in his late fifties, a charming and surprisingly self-effacing man, despite the fact that he must be rich as Croesus. Martha had liked him from the minute she had met him.

'Ah, Ms Clark. How lovely that you are able to come.'

She turned to smile at the small, dark-haired man who was hurrying towards her, both hands outstretched in greeting.

'I'm delighted to be here, Mr Stassinopoulis,' she replied warmly.

'Aristo, please,' he said taking her hands and smiling at her.

'Aristo,' she corrected, 'and please, call me Martha.'

He bowed his head in acknowledgement, then led her into a long room filled with people, introducing her to so many that soon her head was spinning. Several of the names she had heard before and could place them as influential people in the city, yet Martha found them easy to talk to, found that they were intrigued by her profession. She moved round the room, enjoying the chance to meet new people and share a few hours with them. It had been ages since she'd last done this sort of thing and, suddenly, she realised just how much she missed it. It was high time she started to make a life for herself away from the business.

After a while it became very hot in the room, and Martha finally excused herself from the group she was with, making her way through the throng to where drinks were being served at a long, white-clothed table. She opted for a glass of iced fruit juice, wanting something to quench her thirst, then wandered over to the doorway to the ballroom while she watched the couples dancing.

The women's dresses made vivid splashes of colour against the formal dark suits of their partners, and Martha watched them for several minutes, enjoying the shifting flow of colours and patterns this human kaleidoscope was making.

'You're looking very lovely tonight, Martha.'

The shock of hearing his voice was so great that Martha dropped the glass, watching with disbelief as it fell to the floor, spraying cold drops of juice over her sandalled feet. She looked round, her eyes huge and haunted as she stared at the tall, golden-haired man standing beside her.

'What are you doing here? How dare you follow me?' she said furiously, her face pale and tight with anger and a shadow of fear. 'How dare you?'

The music stopped abruptly and Martha felt her face suffuse with colour as the sound of her voice carried round the room. There was a momentary lull in the conversation and she could almost feel people watching them, then a woman laughed, the band once again started to play, and everyone carried on as though nothing had happened.

Quinn Maxwell took her arm, his fingers hard as they closed round her soft flesh, his face a golden mask of barely controlled anger. He nodded towards a waiter, indicating that he should clear up the mess from the spilled drink, then hustled Martha unceremoniously from the room, holding her arm so tightly that she couldn't break free without causing a scene.

'Let me go!' she ordered, her voice a biting, icy whisper, but he ignored her.

Crossing the wide hall, he thrust a door open and bundled her inside the room, closing the door firmly before he freed her. Martha shot away from him like a rabbit from a trap, not stopping till there were several yards between them, her arms hugged tightly round her shaking body. She opened her mouth, ready to tell him in no uncertain terms what she thought of his latest move, but fell silent as he held up his hand to forestall her.

'Just for once, listen, will you? For your information, I didn't follow you here tonight. I was invited. I had no idea that you would be here until I saw you standing by the ballroom.'

'I don't believe you. It's just another one of your rotten tricks, Quinn Maxwell. I bet you gatecrashed this party just to upset me.' She was so angry that she could feel herself quivering, but she forced herself to stand and face him squarely.

'Oh, come on, Martha. Use your head. How could anyone gatecrash a party like this? That guy who let you in isn't some nice old family retainer, he's one of Aristo's bodyguards, same as most of the waiters. If I'd attempted to gatecrash this little do, I'd have found myself out on the pavement with a few bruises for my efforts.'

His words made sense, too much sense, and Martha stemmed the flood of nasty comments which were waiting to erupt like red-hot lava. Her host was an important man; there was no way he would take a chance on strangers walking into his home. For once, she seemed to have misjudged him.

She smoothed her dress down, then flicked a

few loose curls from her cheek, knowing she should really apologise for what she'd said, yet knowing there was no way she would do so! It had been such a horrible shock to hear his voice and see him standing there that she could feel her insides still quivering from it.

'Nothing to say for yourself now, then? Cat got your tongue?' he asked mockingly, and she glared at him.

'I wish a cat would get you, a nice big one, which would carry you off, far away from me forever.'

'Now, I'm sure you don't mean that, sweetheart, especially not when you're looking so demure in that dress. No woman who looks as beautiful as you do tonight could possibly be harbouring such evil thoughts.'

There was an open admiration in his face now, mingled with the teasing mockery, and Martha glanced away, filled with confusion. Insults and anger she could handle, but compliments were a different matter.

'Look, Martha, I was invited here tonight the same as you were, so we have two ways of handling this situation.'

'What do you mean?' She barely glanced at him, her whole body rigid with a tension she couldn't explain.

'I mean that we can either both stay and make the best of it, or one of us can leave.'

'I have no intention of leaving. I was here first and I am staying.'

He sighed, a fleeting hint of regret on his face as he heard the unbending harshness to her voice. 'Then it looks as if I'll have to do the gentlemanly thing and go, doesn't it?'

He swung round on his heel, reaching for the doorknob when Martha suddenly spoke. 'No. Wait!'

The words burst from her lips involuntarily. She hadn't known she was going to say them, and now she felt herself go hot all over as she realised what she'd done. She swallowed hard, trying to find some moisture for her dry mouth, wondering what had made her do it. Why hadn't she just let him go? It should have been the simplest thing in the world to do—yet, somehow, it wasn't.

'You don't have to leave. Can't we just pretend that we've not seen each other and both enjoy the party?'

'No, I'm afraid we can't. There's no way I can pretend I haven't seen you. I'm too aware of you, and I think you are too aware of me also.'

His voice was soft and deep, and Martha felt her pulse leap then race in a strangely erratic manner. She glanced down, twisting the soft folds of her dress between her nervous fingers.

'I'm right, aren't I?' he asked gently.

She nodded, knowing it was the truth. There was no way she could pretend he wasn't there, could stay at the party and not be aware of him every single second. He knew it, and so did she.

He held his hand out, palm upwards, towards her. 'Then do you think we can call another truce, just for tonight, and pretend that we've only just met and found we like each other's company?'

'Can we?' she whispered, her eyes huge in her pale face.

'Yes—yes, I think we can, Martha, if we both want to. I'm willing to try, but are you?'

She hesitated, her eyes tracing over his face, every nerve in her body sending out warning signals. He was a ruthless womaniser, a gigolo, who knew every trick in the book, plus a few not even written, about playing on a woman's emotions. She would be a fool to agree, yet all the warnings seemed to be falling on deaf ears.

She walked forwards, sliding her fingers slowly into his, feeling the hard warmth of his hand with a tingling surge of awareness.

'Yes, I'm willing, Quinn, just for tonight.'

He smiled at her, his face gentle. 'Just for tonight, then, Martha.'

The words sounded like a promise.

CHAPTER EIGHT

THE band was playing a slow waltz, and Martha sighed, her body swaying gently to the dreamy rhythm.

'Tired?'

The low-voiced question rumbled close to her ear, and she turned her head, a soft smile curving her lips.

'Just a little, but pleasantly so.'

'It's been a lovely evening, hasn't it?' Quinn asked quietly, his grey eyes staring deep into hers.

'Yes, lovely,' she echoed, and turned her face away before he could read too much in her expression.

He pulled her closer, his arms crossed low round her back, easing her against the hard strength of his tall body, and Martha gave herself up to the sheer pleasure of resting against him and let herself drift in time with the music. They had danced nearly every dance throughout the night, from the fast, up-beat tempos which had brought a flush of colour to her face and surge of excitement to her blood, to this slow and utterly sensuous waltz. Deep down she knew she should really set some distance between them, should move away from the disturbing feel of his body brushing against hers,

146

but she just couldn't. A strange languor seemed to have invaded her body, making her content to stay where she was in his arms.

With a final flourish the music ended and couples started to walk from the floor. The crowd was thinning out as guests left the party, and Martha knew that the time had come for her to make a move also. She pulled herself free of the arms which were still holding her, and stared up into Quinn's handsome face, her green eyes holding a trace of sorrow she couldn't quite hide.

'I suppose I'd better be going home now. It's very late, and I have work in the morning.'

As though to reinforce her claim, a clock chimed, sweetly proclaiming midnight, and Quinn smiled, his face teasing.

'Twelve o'clock, is it, Cinders? Afraid your coach is going to turn back into a pumpkin?'

Martha laughed, leading the way across the ballroom, aware of the warm pressure of his fingers at her waist.

'Well, I don't know about a pumpkin, but my little Metro won't be too pleased about being left standing out in the cold, I can tell you. She's very temperamental about icy weather.'

'How about letting me drive you home?' he asked, drawing her to a halt in a quiet corner of the room. 'I don't like the idea of you driving alone at this time of the night.'

He caught her hands and Martha glanced down at their linked fingers, overwhelmed with a desire to agree just to prolong the evening. It had been so wonderful, better than any night she could remember, and she didn't want it to end, but it had to.

'No, there's no need, really. I'll be perfectly all right. I'm well used to looking after myself.'

She was unaware of the faintly wistful note which crept into her voice, but the man standing quietly watching her wasn't. He reached out and ran a long finger down her cheek, brushing the velvety softness of her skin in a light touch which trickled fiery sensation through her body.

'I'm sure you are, Martha, but I'd feel much better knowing you were home safely.'

The touch of his hand against her skin was making her breathless, and for a second Martha could only stand and stare at him, her eyes reflecting her inner turmoil.

'I . . .' She got no further as he leant forwards, bending his golden head to press his mouth gently to the parted softness of hers.

'No arguing. Just indulge me in this, sweetheart, please.'

His voice was deep, his grey eyes soft as velvet, and Martha couldn't find the strength to argue. She nodded, then turned quickly away, feeling her heart racing. She was playing with fire, she knew, because tonight, during the hours they'd danced and talked, she had finally accepted something she'd been fighting almost from the beginning: that, despite everything, she was attracted to Quinn Maxwell. The knowledge terrified her.

A maid fetched Martha's coat, then they joined

the queue of departing guests to say their goodbyes
to their host. Aristo took her hands, then kissed her
on both cheeks, his dark eyes sparkling with
mischief as they moved from her to Quinn,
standing beside her.

'So, my little Martha, the evening has been a
success, yes?'

Martha blushed a hot, rosy pink as she grasped
his meaning, and Quinn chuckled wickedly as he
noted her reaction. She shot him a quelling look
before replying as calmly as she could manage. 'It's
been a lovely party, Aristo. Thank you. I've really
enjoyed it.'

'And I have enjoyed having you here. You must
come again, and bring Quinn with you.'

'We'll hold you to that, Aristo,' Quinn said,
shaking the smaller man's hand. 'Thank you.'

They left, moving from the warmth of the hall
into the frosty chill of the night. It was snowing,
big, soft, fat flakes, and Martha shivered as they
settled on her heated skin. She pulled the collar of
her coat around her throat, turning automatically
towards her car.

'This way. I'm parked over here.' He caught her
arm to guide her across the snow-slick drive, but
Martha hung back, filled with a sudden fear. Inside
it had seemed the most natural thing in the world to
agree to let him take her home, but now, with the
cold chill of the night making her come to her
senses, she was no longer certain. If she let him
drive her home, then what would happen next?
Would he ask to come in to her flat, and would she

let him? Suddenly a writhing snakepit of worries opened before her and she was no longer certain that it was a good idea. In her present, highly vulnerable state, could she rely on herself to behave sensibly?

'What's the matter?'

He was watching her, his eyes faintly puzzled, his face shadowed, and Martha took a deep breath, feeling the ache of loss spear through her body. It was the right decision she was about to make, the most sensible, logical and rational one, yet so difficult.

'I've changed my mind,' she said quietly. 'It seems ridiculous to take you out of your way when I already have my own car here.'

'Cold feet, Martha?' he asked, a knowing note to his voice. Martha thanked heaven for the fact the night's darkness hid her heightened colour.

'Not at all. It's just common sense, that's all.' She laughed, a false, over-bright trill of sound. 'After all, what's the point in you driving me home if I have to come back here in the morning to collect my car? No, this way is far more sensible.'

'And do you really want to be sensible?'

His voice was soft, sheer seduction, and she swallowed hard, knowing that being sensible was the very last thing she wanted to be at that moment! She nodded, not quite meeting his eyes. He laughed, a low, teasing little laugh, which flowed through her like warm wine through water.

'Oh, Martha, what a little liar you are, but it's your decision and I'm not going to try and sway you from it.'

'You're not?' Her voice was high-pitched, her eyes startled that he should give in without a struggle.

'No. You wouldn't thank me for it, and I don't want there to be any more animosity between us than there is already. Our time will come, Martha, and waiting will only make it all the sweeter.'

He reached out, catching hold of her collar, and pulled her towards him, his eyes dark as they stared into hers. Martha knew he was going to kiss her, she could read it in his eyes, but there was no thought of resisting in her mind. He drew her closer and she closed her eyes, waiting for the touch of his lips on hers, her whole body clenched in expectation.

The kiss was gentle at first, a bare brush of his lips against hers, a teasing, tormenting whisper of sensation, and she moved, turning her mouth more fully up to his, needing to feel the full power of his kiss. With a low groan he let go of her collar, his arms going round her body to crush her against him so that she could feel the heavy, urgent pounding of his heart against her breast.

She raised her arms, linking her hands behind his head, her fingers sliding into the smooth, cool hair at his nape, while she drew his mouth down harder on to hers. His lips moved over hers, nibbling and biting at their softness, inviting them to part so that he could deepen the kiss, and Martha gasped as she felt the sensuous velvet softness of his tongue stroke against hers. Trickles of fiery sensation were racing through her body, pounding through her veins like molten lava, making her ache with longing for him; ache with longing for more than just a kiss.

Snowflakes fell on their faces, melted on their skin, chilling their flesh, yet neither felt them, too caught up in the fire and passion of the kiss. Then gently he eased his mouth away, trailing a river of kisses up from the corner of her mouth to the soft, dark curls at her temple, and Martha shuddered, unable to hide her reaction to this assault on her senses. Her heart was pounding, beating almost as hard and as fast as his, yet she felt no embarrassment at letting him know how she was feeling. The kiss had been too right, too perfect, to ever feel ashamed.

'All right?'

The whispered question slowly brought her back to an awareness of the fact that they were standing right in the middle of the driveway. She pulled away, running a shaking hand over her ruffled, snow-dampened curls.

'I must go,' she said, her voice shaky with emotion. He nodded, his eyes unfathomable as they studied her face. She held her hand out towards him in a strangely formal little gesture.

'Thank you for a lovely evening, Quinn. I'm glad we decided to put our differences aside for these few hours.'

'So am I, Martha. So am I.' He took her outstretched hand and turned it over, pressing his lips to the warm flesh of her palm before closing her fingers gently over the spot. 'Take care, won't you?'

She nodded, suddenly too overcome to speak, and hurried to her car. She unlocked the door and slid inside, pausing as she went to fasten her seatbelt, realising that her fingers were still curled round her palm as though holding on to that last gentle kiss. She laughed softly, wryly, and started the engine, wondering if she would ever want to wash her hand again.

She drove carefully back to her flat, keeping her eyes fixed on the road, aware that only part of her was concentrating on what she was doing. The rest of her was still caught up in the magical wonder of the evening. She quelled an impulse to close her eyes and feel again the pressure of his body against hers, hear again the deep softness of his voice, feel again the burning power of his lips. It might be madness and utter folly, but Quinn had fired her blood like no man had ever done before . . . not even Paul.

The sudden realisation shocked her so much that she cried out in dismay, overwhelmed with guilt that she could think such a thing. Paul had been her husband and she had loved him, still loved him. How could she think that another man's kisses had stirred her more than his?

Tears sprang to her eyes and she brushed them away, but they kept coming. It was as though the dam she'd built inside her when Paul died had suddenly shattered, and all the pent-up emotions had started to flow. A sob rose to her throat and she clamped her hand over her mouth to stifle the outburst. Her vision was blurring with tears and she closed her eyes to blink them away. When she opened them again she went cold with terror.

Lights were coming towards her, headlights, on the wrong side of the road, racing straight at her. She screamed and wrenched on the wheel, pulling the car sharply over to the side. The tyres hit a patch of ice and she felt the car slew, then start to spin in a slow half-circle as the wheels lost the last of their purchase on the slippery surface. She grasped the wheel, her knuckles white as she tried to drive into the skid and correct it, but it was hopeless.

There was a sickening, grating sound of metal scraping against metal which seemed to last forever, and she was flung forwards, her body jolting painfully against the confining grip of the seat-belt, before the car rolled over and she fell sideways, hitting her head against the door. Pain raced through her temple, a fierce explosion of pain so great that Martha cried out. Lights flashed before her eyes, brilliant, dazzling colours which seemed to blind her, then slowly, mercifully, darkness started to fall.

As though from a great distance, she could hear someone calling her name, his voice filled with fear, but there was no way she could fight the drugging pull of the darkness and answer.

The hospital emergency room was crowded. The recent snowfall on top of the icy conditions had taken its toll, and while Martha had been sitting there three other road traffic accidents had been brought in. She'd been lucky: all she seemed to have suffered were a few minor cuts, a host of bruises and a throbbing headache. Yet, seated on the hard plastic chair, her body racked with lingering shivers of shock, it was difficult to be grateful. She huddled deeper into her coat, clamping her teeth together to stop them chattering, feeling sick.

'Here, put this round you.'

Quinn stood up and took off his dinner-jacket, ignoring her feeble murmur of protest that he would catch cold. He draped it round her shoulders, pulling it tight under her chin, then gathered her into his arms.

'Shh, sweetheart. It's all right. It's going to be fine now.'

'I want to go home.'

Her voice was shaking, thick with pent-up tears, and a grimace crossed his face as he heard it. He raised his hand, gently smoothing the matted curls away from her face, his eyes strangely tender as they looked down into hers.

'You can, Martha. Just as soon as you've seen the doctor. Now, just try and calm down. It's all over. I'm here with you.'

There was a strange note to his voice, a slight tremble which surprised her. Had he been frightened that she'd been really hurt in the accident? If she'd felt better, she would have questioned him about it, but for now it seemed to demand too much effort. She snuggled closer into his arms, feeling the warmth from his body ease into her limbs and chase away the edges of the chill. She still didn't understand how he'd come to be at the scene of the accident; she would have to ask him later. For now it was enough to know that he was here, holding her and making her feel safe once more. She closed her eyes, breathing in the spicy smell of his warm skin, feeling the steady, reassuring beat of his heart under her cheek.

'Martha Clark.'

A nurse called her name and Martha stood up rather shakily, handing the jacket back to Quinn before following her into a curtained alcove. She slipped off her sandals and coat as she was instructed and lay down on the bed, feeling her head start to spin at the change in position. The curtains rattled as the doctor came in, and she summoned up a faint smile for him.

'Well, Miss Clark, how do you feel?'

While he was talking he checked her over, his hands moving impersonally over her body, searching for damage.

'Not too bad, considering,' she answered. 'Just a bit shaken.'

'I don't doubt it. How about your head? Have you a headache, double vision, flashing lights?'

He ran through a list of questions, opening her eyelids wide to check her pupils and feeling round the base of her neck and at her temples for any signs of swelling. When he had finished he helped her upright, smiling sympathetically as she groaned.

'It seems you've been lucky. Not much more than a few Technicolour bruises which should provide a talking point for some weeks to come.'

'And the other driver?' she asked, remembering the glare of oncoming headlights with a sickening surge of memory. 'How is he?'

The doctor's face tightened, a grim look in his eyes.

'Fine. The fact that he was drunk probably saved him. He was so relaxed, he must have rolled with the impact.'

'I see. Well, it seems it could have been worse all round, then.'

'A lot worse. Let's hope the police throw the book at him to make sure he doesn't do it again. Next time everyone mightn't be so lucky. Now, I think I'll let you go home, as long as there's someone to take care of you. I would have preferred to keep you in for observation overnight, in case of concussion, but as you can see we're all but bursting at the seams. I doubt if I could find a bed for you.'

Martha slid into her coat, groaning as she stretched her stiffening muscles.

'That's quite all right, Doctor. I understand. I'd prefer to go home, really.'

The doctor swept the curtain aside and they walked out of the cubicle together.

'Well, as long as you're sure there will be someone there who can keep an eye on you. You shouldn't be alone tonight, Miss Clark, just to be on the safe side.'

'Don't worry, Doctor. I'll stay with her.'

Startled, Martha swung round towards Quinn
Maxwell, her eyes widening.

'Oh, but . . .'

'That's fine, then.' The doctor smiled at them
both, slipping his pen back into the pocket of his
white coat, his mind already on the next patient in
the seemingly endless queue. 'Make sure you
collect an instruction sheet from reception on your
way out. It will give you a few pointers on what to
look out for in case of concussion, but I really don't
think there's much danger of it.'

He walked away and Martha stared after him,
wondering what to do next.

'Come along, then. Let's get you home.'

Taking her arm, Quinn led her across the
crowded waiting area, stopping briefly to collect a
printed sheet from the receptionist. Martha stared
at the paper in his hand, feeling desperate.

'But, Quinn, you really don't need to . . .'

'I do need to, and I have every intention of doing
so. So save your breath, Martha. I'm taking you
home and staying the night, no matter how much
you argue.'

There was a steely note in his voice and, looking
at his set face, Martha knew she was just wasting
her time. Maybe if she'd felt a little stronger she
could have put up a fight, but in her present state of
weakness she didn't have the proverbial cat's
chance. She followed him meekly out of the door,
grateful for the solid strength of his arm encircling
her waist as he guided her to where he'd left his

car. Her legs felt like rubber, all quivery and trembly at the knees, and she doubted that she could have walked the few yards unaided.

He opened the passenger door and put her inside, his hands gentle as he fastened the belt securely round her. He walked round the car and climbed in, resting his head against the steering-wheel as though suddenly tired.

'Hell, Martha, when I saw your car roll like that I . . . I . . .' His voice broke, and Martha felt something inside her leap into life as she heard it. She reached out, running her hand gently over his downbent head, wanting to soothe him.

'It's all right, Quinn. It's all fine now.'

Her words were almost an echo of his earlier ones, and he sat up, a faint smile curving his long lips as he heard them. For one long, timeless moment he stared at her, his eyes tracing slowly over her face as though storing the memory of it, then he said softly, 'Yes. It's all fine now, thank heaven.'

He started the engine and drove slowly out of the hospital while Martha stared out of the window with shocked, disbelieving eyes. He hadn't touched her, hadn't said anything other than those few brief words, but the look on his face had told her more than words could ever do. He cared about her, really cared, and the realisation sent a rush of heat through her whole body.

Quinn took charge immediately they got back to her flat, turning on the heating and making tea as though it was the most natural thing in the world for him to do. Martha sat on the sofa, listening to the sound of him moving round the kitchen, filled with wonder that their stormy relationship had mellowed into this sort of harmony. Naturally he would want to help her when she'd been hurt, but there was more to his concern than just a desire to help: so much more that she was frightened to think about it.

'Here you are. Drink this, then bed.'

He put a mug of hot tea into her hands and Martha sipped it, almost gagging at its sweetness.

'I've put plenty of sugar in. Just the thing for shock,' he said, watching her closely, and Martha drank the lot without a murmur. There was so much concern in his face, so much worry in his eyes, that to make a fuss and refuse seemed churlish.

He took the empty mug from her hand, then pulled her gently to her feet, holding her in front of him. Martha felt her pulse leap, then start to race.

'Don't ever do that to me again, will you? I don't think I could go through what I went through tonight again.'

His voice was deep, his eyes filled with remembered agony, and she smiled at him, suddenly desperate to ease the tension and remove that look of pain.

'No chance. I'm not auditioning for any more stunt-driving jobs, no matter what sort of fee they're offering.'

He chuckled, pulling her gently against him, holding her as though she was made of the most fragile china. 'There's no way I'm going to let you, honey . . . no way. Now, before I give in to my baser instincts, let's get you to bed . . . alone!'

Martha's face flamed at his teasing, realising there was more than a hint of truth to it. If she hadn't been feeling so bruised and shaken, then maybe . . . She carefully blanked out the thought and turned towards the bedroom, stopping as a second thought struck her. She glanced round, her cheeks even more fiery at the request she just had to make.

'Quinn, can you . . . well, can you undo my dress for me, please? I can't lift my arms up properly because of these bruises.'

She waited, her back towards him, her face averted, jumping at the cool touch of his fingers against her skin as he undid the zipper. There was a moment of utter stillness, then she felt the soft touch of his lips against her backbone and shuddered at the exquisite flare of sensation it aroused inside her. For a second his hands tightened round the ends of her shoulders, then he gave her a gentle push away from him.

'Go along, while I still have enough strength to resist temptation.'

There was a husky roughness to his voice which told her all too clearly how strained his control was, yet she didn't hurry as she walked away from him. If he had called her back, she would have gone.

She walked into her room and closed the door, leaning back against its hard wooden panels, her body hot with yearning, her mind filled with

longing. She closed her eyes, fighting down the
desire to go back to him and let what would happen
happen. When she opened her eyes again, the first
thing she saw was the photograph on the bedside-
table, and she gasped, turning her head away from
the evidence of her betrayal.

How could she have forgotten about Paul? How?

Martha turned restlessly in the bed, tossing from
side to side in an attempt to fight off what was
happening. It had been months now since she'd last
had the dream, yet she could still recognise the
onset of it. She twisted round, fighting to break free
from the clinging web of sleep and escape the
horror of the encroaching nightmare, but there was
no way she could do it. It had started now, the first
vivid pictures seeping into her mind, and she
moaned aloud in agitation, knowing all too clearly
what was coming next.

She flung her arm out, knocking the lamp to the
floor, but even the sound of its glass shade
shattering couldn't break the nightmare's hold.
The bedroom door opened and Quinn hurried into
the room, his anxious eyes running over her
writhing figure. She moaned aloud, a pitiful thread
of sound which tore at him, forcing him into action.

'Martha! Come on, wake up. Martha!' He sat
down on the bed to pull her upright, desperate to
wipe the look of terror from her contorted face. Her
eyes opened and stared blankly at him, and he felt
himself go cold at the unfocused depths of her
darkened pupils. He shook her gently, careful not

to jar her head, his hands firm and warm against her cold, damp flesh.

'Martha! Can you hear me? Wake up. You're dreaming. Wake up, I say!'

She blinked, then shuddered, and he pulled her against him, his hands running over her hair, his lips moving desperately over her face.

'It's all right, my love. It's all right.'

Life seemed to flow back into her body and she clung to him, her slender arms gripping him with a surprising strength.

'Oh, thank heaven. You're safe . . . safe.' Her voice was a cracked whisper, an echo of tortured sound, and he bent his head to press his mouth to hers, frantic to wipe away that edge of fear. She lifted her face almost blindly to him, her lips clinging, feverish in their response.

'I love you,' she mumbled. 'Oh, Paul, I love you so much. Don't ever leave me again.' She nestled against him, her body relaxed now, free from the terror, but there was something wrong. He was pushing her away, his hands almost rough as they forced her back against the pillows when she tried to cling to him.

'Open your eyes, Martha,' a harsh voice said. 'Open your eyes and look at me.'

Slowly she opened her eyes and stared up at the tall blond man standing over her, shaking her head to rid it of the last clinging threads of sleep.

'Who am I?'

It seemed such a foolish question that for a moment Martha stared at him, her eyes filled with confusion. Why was he waking her up to ask her such a silly question?

'Who am I, Martha?' he repeated, and his tone dared her not to answer. She licked her dry lips as the first memories of the nightmare came curling back into her mind like drifting smoke, hazy and indistinct.

'Quinn,' she answered. 'Quinn Maxwell.'

'That's right . . . so who the hell is Paul?'

There was anger in his voice now, a real live anger, but she scarcely heard it, too caught up in the horror of the mistake she'd made. She turned away, her eyes going to the photograph, her whole body trembling.

'My husband,' she whispered. 'My husband!'

The echo from the words followed him as he walked out of the room.

CHAPTER NINE

IT WAS almost an hour before Martha summoned up enough strength to leave the bedroom, an hour which she'd spent staring blankly at the wall, her mind and body numb. She walked into the sitting-room and stopped dead, feeling her heart start to hammer in a crazy, frightened rhythm.

Quinn was slumped in one of the chairs, his eyes closed, his head resting back against the cushions, but she knew he wasn't asleep. There was too much tension in his body, too much strain etched on his face for him to be asleep.

She walked further into the room, her bare feet making no sound on the thick carpet, yet somehow he must have sensed her presence. He sat up and ran his hands roughly through his hair, then looked at her, his grey eyes dark and unfathomable.

'How are you feeling?' His voice was politely level and something inside Martha leapt in sudden fear as she heard it. She would almost have preferred to hear anger in his voice than these cool tones of a stranger.

'I'm fine, thank you.' She turned away and stared out of the window, rubbing her hands up and down her cold arms, but the chill she felt stemmed from deep inside and wouldn't go away. The snow had

165

stopped now, leaving behind a thin shimmering coat of white which turned the city street into a magical fairyland, but it wouldn't last. By the morning it would have gone, tainted by the grime and dirt which lay beneath.

There was the sound of movement behind her and she glanced round. Quinn was standing now, shrugging his suit jacket on, and Martha felt herself go even colder as she realised he was leaving.

'Wait! I want to explain about what happened before.'

'Explain? What is there to explain, Martha? I would have thought it was quite obvious what happened.' His voice was harsh, and Martha felt her eyes sting with tears as she heard it. She had hurt him, and no amount of explanations could ever really make up for that, but she had to try.

'But, Quinn, you don't understand . . .'

'No, I don't! I don't understand how you could do this. It's like something out of a farce, isn't it? Any minute now your husband will come in and demand to know what I'm doing here. What's the next step? Pistols at dawn? Well, I'm not waiting round for that to happen. I've had enough, thank you!'

'Paul is dead.'

The words rang round the room, as hollow and final as a tolling bell, and Martha saw the shock which crossed his face.

'What?'

'He died three years ago, in a car accident. I wasn't with him when it happened, but afterwards

I kept having these terrible nightmares, imagining him lying in all that twisted metal.' Her voice broke and she turned away, not seeing how Quinn half raised his hand towards her before letting it drop to his side in an oddly sad little gesture.

'I suppose the accident tonight brought it all back to me, but you must believe me when I say I'm truly sorry I made such an awful mistake. I never meant to hurt you like that.'

'I'm sorry too, Martha,' he said quietly, and his voice held a strange note of defeat. 'I never knew that you'd been married, you see, let alone widowed. It explains so much about you, about the way you reacted to me.'

'What do you mean?' Wide-eyed, she stared at him, seeing the grey strain of tension under his tan.

'Your husband is dead, Martha, but be honest, have you ever really come to terms with it? Isn't he still a part of your life, as important to you as ever?'

Just hours ago she would have agreed with him, but now she wasn't so certain. So much seemed to have changed in these past few hours that it was impossible to know just how she felt. Yet guilt and a strange indecision made her hesitate, and he misread that hesitation.

'You don't need to answer. I can see that I'm right. I'm sorry, Martha, sorry if I've upset you. I never meant to. All I wanted to do was . . .' He stopped abruptly, his face darkening with pain, then slowly turned and walked out of the door. Martha watched him leave with sad and empty eyes, wishing she could call him back, but she couldn't. She had no right to do that.

It was a week before she felt up to returning to work. The bruises were fading, the worst of the stiffness easing from her muscles, but it wasn't really the aftermath of the accident which had kept her at home. It was more a strange reluctance to go out and face the world again.

At the flat she could hide away and lick her wounds, safe from the pain of reality. But it was only a temporary sanctuary. The day came when she knew she had to gather up the threads of her life again, no matter how painful it would be.

She'd seen and heard nothing of Quinn since that dreadful night. He'd walked out of her flat and out of her life, and she missed him, so much that it felt as though he had taken part of her with him when he'd left. How had he managed to become such an essential part of her life, like food or air or water? She didn't know. Yet every minute of every day and every second of every night, she missed him. Was she in love with him? It was a question she'd spent hours puzzling over, but she was still too confused by pain and guilt to know the answer. If she loved him, then how could she still profess to love Paul?

The first day back she walked slowly along the corridor to her office, stopping outside the door to the adjoining suite. Just a couple of weeks ago she'd stood in this very spot, wishing Quinn Maxwell was a hundred miles away; now she would give anything to have him close again. She ran her fingers over the paint, feeling the tiny rough spots where the name-plate had been unscrewed from the door. Jeannie had told her over the phone that he'd closed the office the day after her accident: her voice had held surprise, yet Martha hadn't shared that feeling with her. Quinn had taken the office for one reason and one alone. There was no longer any reason for him to keep it.

With a sigh she walked the rest of the way along the corridor, summoning up a smile at Jeannie's obvious pleasure when she saw her. George Bryant had been holding the fort since she'd been away, and her desk was tidy, the paperwork up-to-date. When she felt better able to think, she would have to consider taking him into partnership with her.

Jeannie followed her into her room, her cheerful face filled with concern as she noticed Martha's pallor.

'Are you sure you're well enough to be here, Ms Clark?'

'Yes. I'm fine, really.'

'Well, you must try and take things easy for a couple of days. George has dealt with most of the new stuff, apart from two clients who insisted on seeing you personally. I've re-booked them for next week.'

'Good. Thank you.'

'And all the current cases have been dealt with, except for this one. George said you wanted to handle this yourself.'

Jeannie eased a folder out of the pile and handed it to her before turning to go, missing the look of shock which crossed Martha's face. She stared down at it, her eyes locked to the name neatly typed along its edge.

So this was it: the end of the case, and the end of her involvement with Quinn. The realisation was like a knife in an open wound. Now all that remained to be done was for her to write her report and pass it on to her clients, yet she knew she couldn't do it. There was no way she could parcel up this list of dates and facts, this slice of Quinn's life, and send it to strangers. She owed him more than that, much more.

She picked up the phone and carefully dialled the number Johnson had left her in case of any problems. She would inform him first and Morris later. It could mean trouble for the business when they found out she had broken their contracts, but that didn't matter. All that mattered was that she should repay this debt she owed Quinn Maxwell.

A secretary put her through to Mr Johnson, and Martha introduced herself, wondering at his barely concealed gasp of horror when he realised who was calling.

'I'm sorry to bother you, Mr Johnson, but I needed to talk to you about your case.'

'My case?' he echoed.

'Yes. I'm afraid that——' She stopped abruptly as he butted in, his voice quivering with agitation.

'Ms Clark, I'm sorry, I've been meaning to contact you, but I . . . well, I really didn't know how to go about it.'

'I'm afraid I don't quite follow you. Is there

something wrong?'

'Well, yes and no.' He hesitated, and Martha had the strangest feeling that he was steeling himself to continue. 'Ms Clark, I want you to drop the case immediately.'

'Drop it?' She was so surprised by his unexpected request that she could only repeat his words inanely.

'Yes, drop it. It appears I have made a dreadful mistake. There was never any question of Margaret being unfaithful to me.'

'I see.' Her head was whirling, trying to absorb the information, but she needed more than this blank statement. 'Can you tell me why you've come to this conclusion?'

'Well, I suppose I really do owe you an explanation. It appears that my wife and her friends met this gentleman, a Mr Maxwell, at a WI meeting. He was giving a talk on investments: stocks and shares, unit trusts, that sort of thing. Evidently the talk was so inspiring that Margaret and three of her friends decided to try their hand at it. Maxwell offered to make the investments for them, but they decided they wanted to do it all themselves. They have been going to his house and, following the advice he's been giving them, have managed to turn their rather modest investment into a tidy little profit. Margaret didn't want to tell me before because she wanted to surprise me with a trip to Venice for our wedding anniversary, paid for out of her share of the profits. So as you can see, Ms Clark, there is no way I want her to know that I doubted her, even for a moment. It would be quite inappropriate.'

'I understand, Mr Johnson, and you can rest assured that the matter will go no further. I'm only glad that it's reached such a happy conclusion.'

Martha made her farewells, refusing his offer to pay for any expenses she'd incurred, and hung up. She sat quietly at her desk, staring down at the file. She should have felt surprised by the revelation, startled that all her suspicions had been so wrong, yet, somehow, she wasn't. Somewhere during this past week she'd begun to realise that Quinn couldn't do such an underhand thing. If only she could have told him that before he left. She had taken an innocent friendship and business arrangement, and turned it into something sordid. She had to apologise to him, yet she knew she couldn't bear to face him again just yet.

She ran her fingers lightly over the smooth, thin card, and suddenly it came to her exactly what she must do. She must send this whole file to Quinn, unopened, unread, and let him decide what to do with it. The best place for it now was the back of the fire!

She rang through to the courier service she occasionally used for urgent letters, then busied herself sealing the file into a thick envelope while she waited for it to be collected. When the driver came she handed it over and gave him strict instructions that it should be delivered to Quinn Maxwell personally, and no one else. There was no way she wanted this little time-bomb to go astray!

She settled down and started to work, trying hard to force aside the strange feeling of restlessness which filled her. Usually she enjoyed her work so much, yet today she found it difficult to concentrate on even the simplest task. Her thoughts kept wandering this way and that, before sliding back along a familiar path to Quinn. How she missed him!

There was a tapping at the door and Martha looked up, glad of the interruption.

'Yes, Jeannie. What is it?'

'This package, Ms Clark. I'm afraid the driver has had to bring it back.'

She held the neatly sealed packet out to her and Martha felt her stomach lurch in shock.

'Why?' she asked, her voice tight with the control she'd placed on it. 'Wouldn't Mr Maxwell accept it?'

She took it from the girl's hands and laid it back down on her desk, snatching her hands away as though it would burn her.

'Oh, no, nothing like that. It seems Mr Maxwell has gone away—back to Australia, so one of the neighbours said.'

She left the room and Martha stared down at the packet with tears in her eyes. He'd gone away, set the whole of the world between them. That really and truly was the end of the whole affair.

CHAPTER TEN

THE days slipped past, Christmas came and went, and Martha tried hard to get on with her life again, but it was difficult when things seemed to have changed so much. The business which had once been all-important seemed less so. It was still a major part of her life, but no longer enough to fill it. Just after the New Year she made her offer of a partnership to George Bryant and he accepted. It meant she had more free time on her hands than she'd had for ages, time she tried to fill by building a social life for herself. Yet no matter how marvellous the play, how delicious the dinner, how stimulating the company, there was always something missing, and that something was Quinn Maxwell.

She loved him. There was no longer any way she could deny the fact or deceive herself into believing otherwise. She loved him with all her heart and soul, yet she could never tell him when there were all those miles between them.

One night she dined at Aristo's house and spent the whole evening remembering the last time she'd been there with Quinn. Everywhere she turned there seemed to be reminders of him, of how they'd talked, how they'd danced . . . how he'd kissed her.

It was sweet agony to remember those hours. She went home after dinner and sat on her bed for hours, staring at the photograph of Paul. For all these years she had tried to hold on to him, to keep her love for him vital and alive by denying her own feelings, but there was no longer any way she could continue to do it. She couldn't spoil everything they'd shared by living a lie. She had loved Paul and would always keep a special place in her heart for him, but now time had done its healing. She could look back on her love for him without regret, without guilt, and place it gently aside while she made a new life for herself. In her heart, she knew it was what he would have wanted her to do.

She wrapped the photograph in a layer of tissue paper and placed it gently in a drawer, no longer needing it beside her bed as a constant reminder. In her heart, Paul would always be alive. It gave her some measure of peace to finally come to terms with the fact, to take that first hardest step out of the shadows. If only she could have Quinn back in her life, then everything would be perfect. But this was real life, not a fairy-tale, and that could never happen.

January raced past, cold and dismal, followed by a blustery February, and Martha knew she just had to get away for a break. The events of the winter had taken their toll, and she needed some time to try and get herself together again. She loved Quinn, she always would, but there was no future in it and she couldn't let it destroy her life completely. It had been a long, hard struggle for her to get this far; she couldn't allow herself to slip back.

She stopped off at the travel agent's after lunch one day and arrived back at her office, her arms filled with glossy brochures, her mind awash with exotic places. The Bahamas, Bermuda . . . the choice was endless. The only blight on the whole venture was that she wouldn't be able to share it with the man she loved. Humming softly to herself, she elbowed the office door open and staggered inside, scattering brochures in a shiny wake across the pale grey carpet.

'Oh, damn! Can you get them for me, please, Jeannie? Jeannie!'

With a cry of alarm she dumped the whole pile into one of the armchairs and crossed the room to catch her secretary by the shoulders, her eyes filled with concern as she saw the girl's shocked pallor.

'Here, sit down.'

She tried to push Jeannie into a chair but the girl resisted, freeing herself from Martha's hold and all but wringing her hands together in consternation.

'Oh, Ms Clark, I'm so sorry. I only slipped out for a minute, to get a sandwich. I know I should have locked the door, but I thought Mr Bryant was in the office. Oh, dear . . .'

Tears welled to her eyes and Martha stared at her in complete bewilderment. What on earth had happened?

'For heaven's sake, Jeannie, it can't be that bad, surely? Pull yourself together and tell me what's happened.'

Jeannie sniffed, then wiped her nose on a

crumpled tissue and pointed towards Martha's office.

'In there, you'll see.'

Martha spun round and hurried towards her room, wondering what she would find, but nothing could have prepared her for the sight which met her eyes. Roses . . . dozens and dozens of pale yellow roses, massed in vases, baskets, urns, on every available surface. For a moment she stood transfixed, her head reeling from the shock and the heady perfume of the delicate flowers.

'I . . .' Her voice dried up and she swallowed hard, trying to ease the tension which suddenly gripped her. 'Who brought them, Jeannie?' Her voice was a bare whisper, yet she felt as though she'd screamed the words aloud.

'I don't know, Ms Clark. I'm really sorry, but they were just here when I came back. I didn't see who brought them. Do you have any idea?'

'Yes,' Martha whispered. 'Yes, I think I have.' Once before she'd been sent flowers like these, perfect pale yellow roses: could the man who'd sent them then have sent these now? The idea was so staggering that she sat down abruptly and stared round at the flowers with wide, shocked eyes. If she was right, then it could mean only one thing . . . that Quinn was here. She put her head in her hands, feeling the fine tremor which raced through her body at the thought, making her heart pound and her legs turn to water.

'Martha, I . . . Good lord! What's going on?'

George Bryant stood in the doorway, his

expression almost comical as he looked at the flowers. Then he grinned, a slow, smug little grin, as though he'd suddenly added two and two, and come up with the perfect answer.

'Well, it explains one thing at least.'

There was a teasing note to his voice, and Martha glanced up at him, wondering what could have brought such a tone to George's usually ultra-correct manner.

'Explains what?'

'Explains what that Maxwell chap is doing standing in the newsagent's doorway across the street. I was wondering what he was up to.'

For a second Martha thought she would faint, as a wave of dizziness hit her. She clung hold of the desk, her fingers digging painfully into the hard wood.

'Are you sure?'

'Quite sure. Take a look yourself.'

Her legs felt boneless, but somehow she forced herself to her feet and walked to the window, pushing the blind aside to peer out into the street.

He was standing exactly where George had said he was, wearing the same leather jacket and jeans she'd seen him wear before, his blond hair tossing wildly in the icy wind. For a long second Martha just stared at him, wondering if he was real or a figment of her overwrought imagination. Yet nothing on this earth could have looked as beautifully real as he did at that moment!

Dropping the blind, she ran from the room, brushing past George and a startled Jeannie, terrified he would disappear before she got chance to speak with him. Outside it was pouring, a heavy, cold rain which soaked her clothes in seconds, but she didn't even notice it as she stood out on the pavement.

'Quinn!' She wasn't conscious of calling his name, but she must have because he looked up, his body tensing as he caught sight of her. He took one slow step forwards, then another, then held out his arms—and without another thought Martha raced across the road and flung herself into them.

'Quinn! Oh, Quinn!' She couldn't seem to find anything to say other than his name, but it was enough. He hugged her to him, his arms holding her so tightly that she was crushed against his body. For one long moment he stared down into her wet face, his eyes like silvery fires, burning with an emotion which made her breath catch and her heart leap in a crazy, joyful rhythm.

'Oh, Martha, I don't know how I've managed to stay away from you so long.'

He bent his head and kissed her, his lips cold and wet with rain, yet burning with a desire he couldn't hide. Martha kissed him back with all the pent-up love she'd held in check these long and lonely weeks.

Finally he drew away, resting his forehead against hers, his big body shuddering with emotion.

'This isn't how I'd planned it, Martha. I wanted our first meeting to be so perfect. I'd even come up with a nice, romantic speech about did you feel able to leave the shadows and come into the sunlight with me, but I guess the weather has put paid to that.' He cast a wry glance at the leaden sky and Martha laughed, snuggling closer into his arms.

'I don't need any fancy speeches, Quinn. I just need to hold you and have you hold me. That's enough.'

'Is it? Don't you even want to know if I love you?' His voice was deep and Martha raised her face to his, her green eyes filled with a desperation she couldn't hide.

'Do you?' she asked. 'Do you love me, Quinn? Because I love you.' Maybe she should have held back, waited until he'd answered, but this was no contest, no attempt to score points off each other. She loved him and she wanted him to know it; it was all that mattered.

Spasms of shock passed through him as he heard her words, and he drew her closer, pressing her body against his as though terrified she would suddenly disappear.

'Do you, Martha? Are you sure?' There was such desperation in his voice, such a need for reassurance, that Martha felt something tender flare to life inside her. She raised herself on tiptoe and pressed her lips to his as she whispered softly, 'Yes, quite sure.'

'Thank heavens! I love you so much, but I didn't dare hope that . . .' His deep voice broke and he pressed his cheek to hers, holding her close.

'*Excuse* me!' An elderly woman pushed past them, glaring her displeasure that they were blocking the doorway to the shop. With a murmured apology Quinn pulled Martha aside, his expression wry as he studied her soaked hair and clothes.

'Let's get out of here, shall we, before we get arrested for obstruction or something worse?'

Martha laughed and clung to his hand as they hurried along the street to his car. Inside, Quinn turned to her and kissed her hard, just once, but it was enough, like the seal on an unspoken promise. They drove in silence to his house and he let them in, forcing the rain-swollen door open with his shoulder. Martha looked round in surprise at the dust-sheets shrouding the furniture, the stack of leaflets behind the hall door.

'Haven't you been home yet?'

'No. I picked up the car, then came straight round to your office. I didn't want to waste any more time before seeing you. It's been too long already.'

He reached out and caught her shoulders, his hands running down her back to mould her against the full length of him, and Martha trembled as she felt the tension in his body. She lifted her arms and twined them round his neck, holding him tightly, never wanting to let him go again.

'I missed you, Martha,' he said softly, and his eyes spoke volumes of the torment he'd suffered.

'I missed you, too,' she answered, and knew she would spend the rest of her life making up for that suffering if he would let her.

He bent his head and kissed her, slowly, deeply, a

kiss of such love and tenderness that Martha felt tears start to her eyes. When he raised his head, she sniffed loudly and he looked at her with concern as he saw the sparkling drops on her lashes.

'Hey, what's all this for?' He brushed his fingertips gently over her eyelids, wiping away the tears, and Martha smiled at him, a shaky little smile.

'It's just that I'm so happy to see you. I thought I'd never . . .' Her voice broke and he crushed her to him, his arms holding her so tightly that she could feel the steady thud of his heart as though it was her own.

'I know, my love. I know exactly what you mean. There's a lot we have to talk about, but not yet. You need to get out of those wet clothes before you catch a chill. I don't want my future bride laid up with pneumonia, now, do I?'

'Your future bride,' she echoed, her face colouring at the expression in his eyes. He laughed and pushed her gently along the hall.

'Go on, that's an order. Get yourself out of those wet things while I light the fire in the sitting-room.'

With waves of delicious excitement racing through her, Martha walked through to the bedroom and stripped off her sodden clothes, praying he hadn't been teasing. His bride . . . the idea was almost more than she could bear. She towelled herself dry, then slipped on one of Quinn's robes she found hanging behind the door, rolling the trailing sleeves up several inches and fastening the belt tightly round her waist before walking quietly to the sitting-room.

Quinn was sitting by the fire, feeding logs to the glowing flames. The firelight danced over his golden hair, deepening it to a burnished sheen, and Martha stopped in the doorway, drinking in the sight. It was one she would hold in her heart forever. He glanced up and smiled when he saw her, holding his hand out towards her, and she went and sat down on the floor beside him, resting her head against his knees.

'Feel better now?' he asked, running a gentle hand over her damp hair. She nodded, then felt herself grow tense as he spoke again, a serious note in his deep voice.

'There are a few things I think we should clear up first, don't you?'

'What sort of things?' She drew away, her body stiff with sudden apprehension.

He pulled her back, his hand smoothing down her cheek in a light caress.

'About what I do for a living for starters, and about Paul. I want us to build a new life together, sweetheart, but there must be no secrets between us, no shadows from the past. I know it might be painful for you to talk about him, but it has to be done.'

'It's not painful, Quinn, not any longer. You see, I've finally done what I should have done years ago, and let him go.' She looked up, her eyes very clear in the firelight. 'I loved Paul. We met when we were both very young and he was as much a friend to me as a husband. It was a tragedy that he should have died like that, but I've finally accepted it. I felt almost guilty that I was still alive, felt I would be betraying him if I fell in love ever again, but now I know that was wrong. He will always be a part of me, Quinn, you have to understand that, but the gentle love I felt for him is nothing like this fierce love I feel for you.'

A wave of relief seemed to wash through him, and Martha knew he had been steeling himself against the pain of her answer.

'Do you know, I've been dreading asking you about him. I've spent hours brooding over it. You see the main reason I left was because there was no way I could fight a ghost for your love. I felt so utterly helpless in the face of the hold he still had over you.'

'I understand.'

'I think I started to fall in love with you almost from the beginning; I know you made me furious with your prying and meddling! I was determined to make you admit that you were wrong about me, to get under your skin in such a way that you'd really have to stop and think. But very soon I realised that I had other reasons for seeing you. I began to enjoy our little skirmishes, to look forward to them as an excuse to be with you, but it took that accident to really ram home to me just how deeply involved I was becoming.'

'How did you come to be there that night? I never did get the chance to ask you.'

'Well, after you'd refused to let me drive you home, I knew I wouldn't be able to rest until I knew you were safe. I followed you, and when I saw that car coming round the bend on the wrong side of the road . . . It was a good job they had to cut the driver out of his car, I can tell you. I think I could have happily killed him for what he did to you. I've never been so scared before in the whole of my life.'

There was remembered agony in his voice, and Martha swivelled round to take his hand in hers, tracing a gentle pattern over its tanned surface.

'That was the worst night of my life, Martha. First the accident, then the shock of finding out about your husband. In the space of a few hours I saw all my newly fledged dreams shattered. I decided to go back to Australia and forget about you but, as you can see, I wasn't successful. You were already in my heart and in my blood, Martha. There was no possible way I could make myself forget, no matter how hard I tried. But one thing you must understand is that I was never at any time involved with Margaret, or anyone else, in the way you imagined.'

'I know,' she said quietly. 'After you left I realised that I couldn't carry on with the case, so I rang Johnson up and he told me what had been going on, that you had been advising his wife and her friends on some investments. The strange thing was that it didn't come as a shock. Somewhere along the line I'd already realised that I'd been wrong and that you weren't capable of doing such a dreadful thing.'

'Thank you. It's a relief to hear it, and I know my

mother will feel the same way too.'

'Your mother?' Dumbstruck, Martha could only stare at him, seeing the laughter lying deep in his eyes.

'Now, don't sound so surprised, my love. Even gigolos have mothers, you know. Surely you remember mine . . . the lady at the gallery who was so dead set on buying me that painting.'

'That was your mother? I thought . . . Oh, Quinn, you can't possibly let her know what I believed about you. She'll never forgive me!' Martha jumped to her feet, her face flaming at the very idea.

'Well, maybe I won't . . . just yet.'

'What do you mean "just yet"?' Hands on hips, she glared down at him.

'Well, if you agree to my terms, Ms Clark, then I really don't see any need to tell her what a dreadful mistake you made.'

'Why, that's blackmail!' she declared hotly.

He grinned up at her, his lips curved into an utterly sensuous smile which raised Martha's blood pressure several notches just to see it. 'You're right, of course, honey. It is blackmail, sweet, delicious blackmail, but then, you haven't heard the terms yet. You might like them.'

'What are they?'

'That you marry me, immediately, to buy my silence. What do you say?'

It was the answer to every one of her prayers, and Martha smiled at him, her face alight with joy.

'Yes . . . oh, yes, please, Quinn.'

'Are you sure, now? I mean, I have to be quite certain that you fully understand the terms of the deal, be utterly convinced about it.'

Reaching out, he caught hold of the tie-belt of the robe to pull her down on to his knees, and Martha nestled against him, her lips just a hair's breadth away from his as she whispered softly, 'Just give me a minute, then I'm sure you'll be well and truly convinced!'

Harlequin Presents®

Coming Next Month

#1351 ONE-WOMAN CRUSADE Emma Darcy
When Noah Seton takes over Toni's stepfather's company and dismisses twenty-seven people, Toni Braden decides to fight back. Everyone thinks she'll be no match for Noah—but they haven't counted on Toni's rather unorthodox ideas....

#1352 THE MUSIC OF LOVE Kay Gregory
Belinda truly doesn't mind that she's twenty-six and has never been kissed. Then Hal Blake jogs into her life and shows her just what she's been missing.

#1353 SO CLOSE AND NO CLOSER Penny Jordan
Rue decides to opt for the solitary life and is perfectly content—until Neil Saxton comes along. He's a demanding and dangerous man, so why does she miss him whenever he's not around?

#1354 INDISCRETION Anne Mather
Abby had loved Jake, but she'd lost him—and also Dominic, their child. Now Jake needs her. It's Abby's one chance to restore their relationship—if she can just find the strength to use the situation to her advantage.

#1355 BARGAIN WITH THE WIND Kathleen O'Brien
Darcy's only chance to save her business and her young sister from her lecherous stepfather's control is to get married—so she decides to accept Evan's repeated offer of marriage. But when she turns up in Florida, Miles Hawthorne, Evan's older brother, takes over the decision making!

#1356 AGAINST ALL ODDS Kay Thorpe
Brad Halston had pushed Kerry out of his personal life four years ago. Now he wants her out of his working life, too. But Kerry grew up during those years—and she isn't about to be pushed anywhere....

#1357 LORD OF MISRULE Sally Wentworth
Verity Mitchell simply planned to accompany her widowed friend, Paula, to meet Paula's in-laws in the country. Falling for Sebastian Kent is unexpected—and brings complications when Paula's life is threatened and Verity feels Sebastian is involved.

#1358 SHADOW ACROSS THE MOON Yvonne Whittal
Even after Anton de Ville tries valiantly to dispel Sarah's fears about marriage, she can't bring herself to accept his proposal. She loves him, but the misery of a past bad marriage makes Sarah wonder if she dares to love again....

Available in April wherever paperback books are sold, or through Harlequin Reader Service:

In the U.S.
P.O. Box 1397
Buffalo, N.Y.
14240-1397

In Canada
P.O. Box 603
Fort Erie, Ontario
L2A 5X3

Coming soon
to an easy chair near you.

FIRST CLASS is Harlequin's armchair travel plan for the incurably romantic. You'll visit a different dreamy destination every month from January through December without ever packing a bag. No jet lag, no expensive air fares and *no* lost luggage. Just First Class Harlequin Romance reading, featuring exotic settings from Tasmania to Thailand, from Egypt to Australia, and more.

FIRST CLASS romantic excursions guaranteed! Start your world tour in January. Look for the special **FIRST CLASS** destination on selected Harlequin Romance titles—there's a new one every month.

NEXT DESTINATION:
GREECE

 Harlequin Books

JTR4

Take 4 bestselling love stories FREE

Plus get a FREE surprise gift!

COMING IN 1991 FROM
HARLEQUIN SUPERROMANCE:

Three abandoned orphans,
one missing heiress!

Dying millionaire Owen Byrnside receives an
anonymous letter informing him that twenty-six years
ago, his son, Christopher, fathered a daughter. The
infant was abandoned at a foundling home that
subsequently burned to the ground, destroying all
records. Three young women could be Owen's long-
lost granddaughter, and Owen is determined to track
down each of them! Read their stories in

#434 HIGH STAKES (available January 1991)
#438 DARK WATERS (available February 1991)
#442 BRIGHT SECRETS (available March 1991)

Three exciting stories of intrigue and romance by
veteran Superromance author Jane Silverwood.

Harlequin Intrigue®

A SPAULDING & DARIEN MYSTERY
by Robin Francis

An engaging pair of amateur sleuths—Jenny Spaulding and Peter Darien—were introduced to Harlequin Intrigue readers in #147, BUTTON, BUTTON (Oct. 1990). Jenny and Peter will return for further spine-chilling romantic adventures in April 1991 in #159, DOUBLE DARE in which they solve their next puzzling mystery. Two other books featuring Jenny and Peter will follow in the A SPAULDING AND DARIEN MYSTERY series.